"Come a little closer to your hot date here," West urged

He reached out and took her hand.

"You're my employer, not my date." Mallory was making only a token resistance. His touch was already making her weak, spurring her desire.

She didn't make herself get up and leave. Instead, she put all the no's out of her mind. Why should it matter that West was bare to the waist, only wearing pajama bottoms? It didn't. Tonight, she was brimming with urges to say yes to everything she wanted. Tonight, West was welcome to tempt her into misbehaving.

"Live in the moment," he murmured and rose from the patio chair, drawing her up with him. "It's not such a big sin. Why don't you try it?"

She nodded, willing to let herself go with him.

With an unreadable gleam in his eye he led her by the hand to the fountain. To her surprise, he stepped into the knee-deep water. Kicking up a splash, he grinned. "Come on in. The temperature's just right for a water fight."

Roseanne Williams couldn't resist writing a book about a butler. She loves the idea of having an efficient, unflappable aide-de-camp who anticipates every need—and who even irons the wrinkles out of the morning newspaper! She researched her story by reading about Ivor Spencer's famous butler school in London, where potential butlers must master eighty-six lessons before they are fit to graduate. Although the butler is traditionally thought of as a "gentleman's gentleman," Roseanne turns this idea on its head by having a female butler as the heroine of *Hot Date!*

Roseanne has been nominated as a RITA finalist by the Romance Writers of America for her bestselling Temptation novel *The Bad Boy.*

Books by Roseanne Williams

HARLEQUIN TEMPTATION
384—UNDER THE COVERS
401—THE BAD BOY
427—SEEING RED
443—MAIL ORDER MAN

HOT DATE

ROSEANNE WILLIAMS

Harlequin Books

TORONTO • NEW YORK • LONDON
AMSTERDAM • PARIS • SYDNEY • HAMBURG
STOCKHOLM • ATHENS • TOKYO • MILAN
MADRID • WARSAW • BUDAPEST • AUCKLAND

Published September 1993

ISBN 0-373-25560-8

HOT DATE

"I CAN'T BELIEVE it's your last day as my butler, Danner. I never thought I'd get married and have to give you up."

"It's all for the best," Mallory Danner reassured Vanessa Eaton, her newly wed employer. "Marriage suits you, and you were the most beautiful bride ever, Mrs. E."

Vanessa chuckled delightedly. "The *oldest* bride ever."

"Lord Eaton doesn't think so," Mallory teased. "He practically shouted 'I do' at the altar."

"So did I, Danner. Living in England as his Lady Eaton will be so exciting." Elegant and slightly arthritic, Vanessa stood up behind her carved rosewood desk and came around it to Mallory. Her brilliant smile dimmed.

"If he didn't have a butler of his own already, you could come along with me. I wish I could leave knowing you and the rest of the staff were set in new jobs."

"We'll all be working again in no time," Mallory said. "Don't worry about us. Enjoy yourself!"

Although sad that the job was ending, Mallory was thrilled for Vanessa, whose whirlwind courtship and wedding had been like a fairy tale come true. Mallory loved fairy tales and from now on would treasure the memory of her boss getting swept off her feet by Kenneth Eaton.

He had proposed to Vanessa the night he'd met her. Up to that moment, Vanessa, a wealthy, widowed socialite in her seventies, had been a traditionalist, reserved in public and private. Upon meeting Lord Eaton, however, she had surprised everyone by tossing restraint and tradition to the wind.

She had accepted his proposal on the spot and immediately put her posh estate up for sale. A week later it had sold. Almost overnight she had gotten engaged and married. Today she'd leave her estate in Atherton, California, fly to London and start a whole new life there as Lady Eaton.

"I hope I get along with m'Lord's butler as well as I did with you, Danner."

"You'll have him eating out of your hand, Mrs. E."

In the course of five years, Mallory had developed a warm affection for Vanessa. Perhaps it was because of the affinity she felt with her. In many ways, she and Vanessa had similar personalities. They were dignified, composed and reserved on the surface, but unexpected surprises bubbled up now and then.

Sometimes Mallory even surprised herself. Like the time she had slid down the banister of the main stairway, thinking no one would see, and Vanessa had caught her. Mallory had been mortified, but Vanessa had surprised her by bursting out laughing. They'd both shared a good giggle together about it afterward.

"I'll miss you, Danner."

"I'll miss you, too, Mrs. E." Mallory gave her a smile from the heart. She had loved managing Vanessa's house and staff. "I wish you every happiness."

"And I," Vanessa said with a twinkle in her eye, "wish that wherever you end up, you'll have a long banister to slide down."

Mallory rolled her eyes. "I'll never know why I did that. The urge just popped out of nowhere."

They shared a last laugh, remembering.

Vanessa sighed. "Thinking back on it now, you and I have spent far too much time being proper and self-contained. Now that I've let go and kicked up my heels, I'm not going to stop. I hope you'll do the same."

"It's a butler's business to be proper and self-contained," Mallory replied matter-of-factly.

"Well, I hope that being a perfect butler—and you are one—won't keep you from finding the happiness I've found." Vanessa gave Mallory's arm an encouraging squeeze. "Don't learn too late that life is too short. Don't bottle yourself up the way I did for too long. Have a lark."

"I have a good enough time as it is, Mrs. E."

Vanessa didn't look convinced and Mallory wasn't sure how to convince her. How could she make it clear that being a butler prohibited a person from being himself or *her*self? A butler's role wasn't to let off steam or let her hair down. Only off the job was it possible to do as she wished.

On her own time, Mallory loosened up by improving her most unusual job skills. Trained to be a bodyguard as well as a butler, she spent most of her days off practicing karate. A licensed pilot, she also put in flying time to keep her flight ratings current. Her vacations had always been spent visiting her family in Tucson, Arizona, a relaxing place.

"Really," she insisted to Vanessa. "I have enough outlets for my free time and energy."

"I hope so." Vanessa looked doubtful for a moment, then continued, "You're certain you don't mind living in the gatehouse until you're either employed again or the escrow closes on the house?"

"I wish you'd let me pay rent for it, Mrs. E. Letting me stay for free is really too—"

Vanessa stopped her with a raised hand. "You deserve a big freebie after saving my jewels last year. And we both know that a vacant estate is a vandal's playground. I can leave worry-free, knowing you're on guard in the gatehouse."

"I'll keep my eye on things," Mallory assured her.

"And I," Vanessa promised, "will keep making job inquiries for you among my friends and acquaintances."

None of whom, Mallory knew, needed or wanted a female butler in her late twenties. Butlers of any age were going out of style, especially in casual California.

Vanessa enveloped Mallory in an affectionate farewell hug. "You've been terrific, Danner. The best butler and bodyguard I've ever had."

"The *only* one you've ever had," Mallory pointed out fondly for the last time.

Vanessa laughed. "Not for long. You have my new address. Write often and keep me posted."

"I will, Lady Eaton. Goodbye and good luck."

A MONTH LATER, Mallory sat facing a harried-looking placement agent at a San Francisco employment firm, the best domestic-help agency on the West Coast. "Nanny, nanny, nanny, housemaid," the agent muttered, reading through a file of employer requests. "Chauffeur, nanny, nanny—" He broke off and sighed. "Would you happen to be qualified for child care, Miss Danner?"

"Qualified but not interested," Mallory stated firmly. "I'm a professional butler. My references are impeccable and I'm highly skilled."

"Highly," he agreed. "It's a rare butler who can pack a pistol on duty as you did for your former employer. You were the talk of the Bay Area last year when you caught that jewel thief in the act. Even so . . ."

"I'm also trained in karate," Mallory reminded him, "and licensed to fly small planes and helicopters."

He sighed. "Still, Miss Danner, demand for butlers has fallen from what it was in the eighties, the decade of greed. The recession has taken a toll, even on seriously rich employers."

"Yes, I know." She knew, too, that demand for female butlers had never been high. The agent wasn't saying it outright, but he was implying it.

"On the other hand," he continued, "demand for capable nannies is soaring."

Mallory shook her head. "I'm the eldest of four children," she explained. "My mother died when I was twelve. My triplet sisters were a year old. Believe me, I've changed my last diaper, spoon-fed my last mouth, sung my last lullaby."

"Hmm. And you still don't wish to relocate out of the Bay Area?"

"Only as a last resort."

"Well, someone in the suburbs or city must need a household manager with your special skills. Soon, perhaps." But he looked helpless and hopeless.

Disheartened, Mallory thanked him for his time and left the office. She'd never been unemployed before, never felt so idle or useless. She stood on the sidewalk, half wishing that she'd been born into a long line of nannies rather than a long line of butlers.

Her father had served San Francisco's elite on Nob Hill. His father had served a California governor. Great-grandfather had begun at Buckingham Palace and immigrated to the White House.

Mallory remembered her father warning, "You won't have an easy time of it. People think *gentleman's gentleman* when they think butler."

"What people think," Mallory had countered, "doesn't stop women from being soldiers, sailors and CEO's."

She hadn't let it stop her from being a butler, although she'd begun to have second thoughts recently about her career. Vanessa's words kept coming back to her: *Life's too short. Don't bottle yourself up.*

For Mallory, that was easier said than done. She tightened the belt of her new gray trench coat and plunged her hands into its deep pockets. A gift from Vanessa, the stylish coat had arrived yesterday in a Harrod's box.

"A London original," Vanessa had written. "Cloud gray to match your eyes, and copper-gold lining to match your hair. Thank you for staying on until escrow closes."

It would close next week and the new homeowner would move in. After that, Mallory planned to live in a residence hotel until a job came up. She would miss the gatehouse and Atherton. As unsure about where she was headed as she was about her future, she crossed Market Street and paused to join a small crowd watching the comic antics of a street mime.

Dressed in a Harpo Marx costume and wig, he opened an imaginary can and stirred the "contents" into an imaginary cooking pot. He inhaled the aroma, tasted his concoction, ladled it into an invisible bowl and placed the bowl on an actual table he'd already set up. He pulled out a real chair and pointed at Mallory.

She took a step back, feeling all eyes turn to her. "No, thank you." Shaking her head, she demurred, "I'm not...er..."

The mime's face crumpled. He shed several invisible tears and went down on his knees, pleading, begging.

"Awwww," the audience sympathized.

Mallory couldn't suppress a grin. *Heck*, she thought, *why not kick up my heels? I'm not on the job. Not right now.*

"Okay," she agreed, sitting in the chair.

Smiling broadly, the mime tooted his bulbous horn and then laid a nonexistent napkin over her lap. After spooning soup from the bowl and politely sipping, Mallory frowned, implying that the flavor didn't quite suit.

The mime went into a tizzy, honking his horn in distress at her displeasure. He feverishly added "salt" and "fresh-ground pepper" and breathlessly awaited her response to a second taste.

Mallory spooned, sipped, swallowed, smiled, then suddenly sat bolt upright. She crossed her eyes, sucked in a strangled breath and clutched at her throat. As she lurched out of her chair, she saw the crowd and the mime start in surprise.

Then everyone laughed and the mime began beeping his horn. He made her take several bows with him before she continued on her way.

Mallory chuckled to herself and pushed away a twinge of discomfort about her uncharacteristic behavior. Goofing off always brought back the guilt she felt over her mother's death. She'd been playing games with the neighbor kids the day Mom had died.

Not now, she told her conscience. She didn't want negative thoughts.

By frolicking with the mime, she had let loose for a change and she wanted to enjoy the feeling. It didn't happen very often.

Seeing three grizzled men huddled around a trashcan ahead, she jaywalked to avoid them, then skirted a stretch of broken glass on the sidewalk.

This wasn't the safest area in San Francisco, but it was midafternoon and she wasn't defenseless. She'd spent all morning at karate practice, keeping in shape for a new job. If only it would materialize.

"Help!"

Mallory halted and looked back. The men she had passed seemed to have heard nothing. They were intent on sharing a bottle of liquor. Had she imagined a scream?

"Helllp!!"

It sounded from an alleyway ahead. A woman screaming. Mallory ran toward the alley. She rounded the corner and saw a burly man push an elderly woman into a recessed doorway. He was grabbing at her handbag.

"Noooo," the woman wailed. "Please . . ."

Mallory doubled her fists. A mugger. She ran straight toward him, yelling, "You! Leave her alone!"

"Get lost, bitch," the man snarled, wrenching the woman's purse from her grasp. He turned and jogged away down the alley.

"Thief!" the woman cried, sinking to her knees.

Mallory rushed to her. "Are you hurt? Are you—"

"My handbag," the woman sobbed.

"I'll get it back," Mallory promised.

Furious, she kicked off her pumps and sped after the thief. He was loping along as if he had nothing to fear. He glanced over his shoulder and taunted her with a just-try-it grin.

Mallory clenched her teeth and sprinted after him. She saw his grin dissolve. He broke into a run, but too late. She outraced him, tripped him, then karate-chopped him into dropping the handbag. One well-aimed knee to his groin flattened him on the pavement. He curled into a fetal position.

Mallory stood over him, poised to chop again if he made a move. "There's more where that came from," she advised breathlessly, "so stay right where you are."

Looking up, she saw a young skateboarder watching from the end of the alley. The boy stepped onto his board and rolled up to her.

"Awesome," he said, tipping the brim of the baseball cap he was wearing sideways on his head. "I'll call the cops from the corner phone if you want."

Mallory managed a thankful smile. "Excellent idea."

"Here." He reached into his coat pocket and pulled out a small canister. "Hold him still with this."

Mallory read the label. "Mace?"

"My mom makes me carry it." He shrugged.

"Thank you." Although relieved, Mallory felt a rush of renewed fury that a child should need a chemical for self-protection on city streets. She aimed it at the man on the ground and warned, "I've always wanted to see a grown man cry. If you'd rather not, don't move."

The boy sped off on his board. Mallory watched him go, her chest heaving as she regained her breath. Her captive had begun a litany of curses.

She warily circled around him to view the other end of the alley where the attack had occurred. The mugger's victim was coming forward, shaking a fist at him.

"Purse snatcher," the woman accused as she bent to pick up her handbag from the pavement. Hugging the purse to her breast, she came to Mallory's side. "You were magnificent, young lady, an avenging angel. Who are you?"

"Mallory Danner. Did he hurt you?"

"Not in the least." The woman adjusted her threadbare tweed coat and smoothed a hand over her disheveled white hair. "I need a shampoo and set more than medical attention. I'm Mrs. Ellinor Cade, Ms. Danner. Thank you for happening by when you did."

"Cade?" the mugger muttered. "You gotta be kidding."

Ellinor glared at him. "I'm not kidding." She looked at Mallory admiringly. "You must be an off-duty policewoman. Just what I needed."

Mallory didn't deny being a policewoman because the label might make her seem more threatening to the mugger.

He groaned. "A cop and a Cade?"

Mallory could understand his dismay. Cade was an old, illustrious name in San Francisco. There was Cade Boulevard. The Cade Foundation. Cade Stadium. A crime against a Cade would have serious consequences, cop or no cop.

"*The* Mrs. Cade?" Mallory inquired politely.

"Oh, yes. I'm the rich-and-famous recluse, in person."

Noting the woman's Katharine Hepburn accent and seeing her blue eyes snap with certainty, Mallory almost believed her. However, her shabby coat, unkempt hair and inexpensive handbag made her claim seem incredible.

"Unfortunately, I'll be front-page news because of this, Ms. Danner. Justice must be served, though." She clucked her tongue, gazing off into the distance. "Hmm. He'll be unhappy that I've gotten in a jam again, won't he?"

Mallory questioned, "He?"

"Third, I mean."

Out of deference to a much older woman—who might well be senile—Mallory politely pretended to understand. *Third. As in one-third? Or third base? Or third after second and first?*

"Yes," said Mrs. Cade decisively. "He'll be as upset as he was when I got lost on Nob Hill yesterday." Her blue eyes clouded for a moment, then cleared and brightened as she focused again on Mallory. "Are you single, by any chance?"

"Well . . . yes."

"Not engaged or spoken for?"

"No. Why?"

"Oh, I shouldn't be nosy, I know. I'm sorry."

The woman was sounding increasingly distracted and disjointed, Mallory thought. "Mrs. Cade" seemed more likely to be an eccentric bag lady than a wealthy recluse.

A siren sounded and a police patrol car careered into the alley. The boy came skating behind it on his board. Two officers jumped out of the car.

Mallory was immediately struck by their appearance. They bore a strong resemblance to an aging basset hound and a perky beagle. Mallory almost lost her composure, but caught herself before she burst out laughing.

What a day. First she'd clowned around with a street mime, and now she was seeing canine cops. If she didn't find a job soon, her active imagination would get her into trouble.

"Who's who, here?" the jowly, sag-eyed cop growled.

The boy pointed at the criminal. "The perp." At the victim. "The mark." At Mallory. "The ninja."

Mrs. Cade nudged Mallory. "What language is that?"

"Street slang, Mrs. Cade." Maybe she really was the famous recluse, Mallory thought. But if she was, why was she out in public?

"What happened?" the senior officer demanded.

Mallory gave him her name and driver's license, and began explaining the situation. "I heard a scream and found this man taking Mrs. Cade's purse from her."

Mrs. Cade put in, "I'm Ellinor Cade, Officer."

"Ellinor Cade," he repeated, exchanging a droll, disbelieving glance with his partner. "You have a piece of ID to show us, ma'am?"

"Not at the moment. But I am the only Ellinor Cade in this city," she insisted.

The junior officer regarded Mallory as if, by association, she lacked credibility. "The kid, here, says you kung-fu'd the suspect," he said, eyeing her dubiously. "How do you know martial arts?"

"Well, I'm a butler—" Mallory cut her explanation short, annoyed that both cops were raising their eyebrows at her reply and exchanging another glance.

"Girls can't be butlers," the boy scoffed.

"Girls can be whatever they wish," Mallory pronounced, handing him his Mace. "Thank you again for this and your help."

Mrs. Cade blinked bright, admiring eyes at her. "You're a butler? And a policewoman, too?"

"Only a butler with bodyguard training," Mallory replied, giving both policemen a challenging look that dared them to refute her.

"Whose butler are you?" Mrs. Cade inquired, appearing intensely interested. "Anyone I'd happen to know?"

"People, please," the senior cop entreated, shaking his head. "Let's give the facts a second go-around. Start all over with who—and what—you are." He pointed his pencil at Mallory. "You first, ma'am."

Mallory squared her shoulders, looked him straight in the eye and gave her name again. "Believe it or not, I'm a professional butler."

"And I," said Mrs. Cade, "will prove my own identity at police headquarters. Take me to the chief himself—immediately!"

2

WESTMORELAND CADE III pushed through double-glass doors into police headquarters. Trench coat flying wide open over his dark business suit, silk necktie sailing over one shoulder, he strode past the desk sergeant to the police chief's inner sanctum.

"He's expecting me," West advised the sergeant. For the second time in two days West had come to collect his aunt from the station. Yesterday she'd left home and gotten lost on Nob Hill. Today she'd been mugged.

West raked his hand through his chestnut hair, at a loss to account for the sudden, drastic change in Aunt Elli's behavior. She had been a recluse ever since her lover's death in an auto accident forty years ago. For decades she had seen and spoken to almost no one but West's mother, West himself and her personal physician, Dr. Ortiz. West's father had died long ago and since his mother had died last year, he and Ellinor had been each other's only family.

Until yesterday, she had refused to venture beyond the boundaries of her stately home in the Pacific Heights section of the city. West thought maybe Dr. Ortiz should test her for Alzheimer's. So far, the doctor had unsuccessfully treated her for clinical depression.

West hated the idea of Alzheimer's affecting his beloved Aunt Elli. More than simply an aunt, she was his godmother, infallible adviser, landlady and tolerant housemate. He'd always been protective of her.

"Mr. Cade!" The portly, ruddy-faced chief rose and leaned over his desk to shake West's hand. Seeing Ellinor seated nearby safe and sound, West breathed a sigh of relief.

"Third, dear, I'm so sorry," said Ellinor, presenting her cheek for West's kiss. "It's such a world out there . . . perps and marks and ninjas. Miss Mallory Danner here is the ninja."

West straightened and looked down at the young woman seated beside his aunt. "Miss Danner," he acknowledged. "How do you do?"

"Fine, thank you. And you, Mr. Cade?"

"I'm calming down."

It was true only in regard to his aunt. Miss Danner herself was causing an instant increase in his heart rate. He'd never seen such deeply gray eyes as hers, like two dark clouds rimmed with sunlight. Her thick coppery hair seemed gilded, too, with a subtle radiance. She wore it pulled back, clamped with a tortoiseshell clip, but he could easily picture it tumbling loose and luminous around her oval face.

"We have her to thank for everything, Third," Ellinor said. "She stepped in and saved me from the perp— that is, the perpetrator. You should have seen the karate kick she gave him."

West nodded, eyeing Miss Danner's shapely calves and slender ankles. She must be stronger than her delicate beauty suggested, he mused.

Glancing up, he saw her cheeks flush in response to his appreciative gaze. Her facial expression was polite and pleasant, but there was a spark of recognition—and a strong hint of ambivalence—in her eyes.

It implied that she knew of his reputation—who didn't?—and wasn't quite sure what to make of a lover boy who, like Warren Beatty, was a legend in his own time. Maybe she read *HotScene*, the magazine that had named West Cade "The Hottest Date in the World" three years in a row. Maybe not, but his romantic exploits had been given so much media coverage that she probably knew the basics.

He switched back to Ellinor. "What were you doing in an alley south of Market Street, Aunt?"

"I was making a trip down memory lane, looking for the old Palace Hotel. I got disoriented and he accosted me."

"Thank God you're all right."

"Yes, thanks to Miss Danner."

"Let's go home, Aunt," West said gently, helping her to her feet. "You've had a long day."

"So have I," Mallory rejoined, smiling sympathetically at Ellinor and rising from her seat. "I should be getting home, too." *Home, such as it is,* she thought with a pang. Vanessa's estate was an empty, lonely place now.

Ellinor consulted her wristwatch. "But we're just in time for happy hour." She glanced from Mallory to West. "Why don't we have a cocktail together? We have so much to discuss—the terms of Miss Danner's employment, the gala costume party I hope to put on with her expert assistance."

"Party?" West repeated, looking perplexed.

Mallory felt baffled, too. *Employment terms? Expert assistance?* Mrs. Cade was sounding raddled again.

"I see I'm getting ahead of everyone but myself," Ellinor said, glancing from West to Mallory. "To begin at the beginning, Third, Miss Danner is an unemployed professional butler. And to make a long story short, I've decided I need one."

West gave Mallory a surprised look. "A butler."

"We aren't all gentlemen's gentlemen anymore," Mallory responded. "Times have changed."

Ellinor smiled. "I obviously need a guardian angel just like you. I owe you so much for coming to my aid."

"Mrs. Cade, you don't owe me a job. I did what was necessary and that's all. I'll be on my way."

"Third, please turn on your devastating charm and make Miss Danner come home and have a sherry with us."

West seemed to have shaken off his surprise and now focused his attention on Mallory with what looked like relish. He winked one crystal-green eye and shot her a sexy, seductive smile.

"Aunt Elli and I owe you one. Besides, we've got a super sherry at home that has to be tasted to be believed." He winked at her again. "A rare amontillado."

Mallory hesitated for a moment, then gave in. "I'd love one."

She told herself that the hopeful light in his aunt's blue eyes had persuaded her. Not West's stupendous smile. But she couldn't ignore the heat she could feel on her cheeks. She took a deep breath.

"Dear, persuasive Third," Elli said approvingly.

More than persuasive, Mallory thought. West Cade was enough to bring any woman's blood straight to the surface, even a self-composed butler's. He was already inspiring fantasies that Mallory had never had before.

No wonder. His provocative grin, sun-streaked chestnut hair and intriguing eyes had cut a legendary swath through female society for more than a decade if all the newspapers, magazines and tabloids could be believed.

Mallory believed them implicitly at that moment. She warned herself to drink only a bit of that sherry and to stop her fluttering heart before taking even a sip. If she let any alcohol go to her head, she might forget that handsome, charming, smooth-as-suede rakes were not her style. Suddenly, though, she wished that they were.

No. She stiffened her tingling spine and resolved that there would be no champagne wishes for her, no caviar dreams, no devil-may-care playboys. Just one small glass of rare amontillado. Then she'd be on her way back to the gatehouse . . . home for another few days.

"I'd like to offer you a ride," West said, "but I'm driving a two-seater."

"I'll follow in my car," Mallory told him.

Leading the way out of the office, Ellinor sighed. "I wish you'd driven your three-seater, Third."

West nodded, his green eyes glinting at Mallory. "So do I, Aunt. Goodbye, Chief, and keep this out of the news if you can."

"Will do, Mr. Cade."

Hot Date

MALLORY FOLLOWED West's sport Mercedes up to Pacific Heights and through the automated security gate guarding Ellinor Cade's drive. The home resembled the Spreckels mansion—venerable, historic and blessed with spectacular views of San Francisco Bay.

"Aunt Elli and I live pretty simply here," West said, leading her inside after Ellinor. "No butler, cook, maid, et cetera. Just a cleaning service once a week."

"Simply" was an understatement, Mallory observed as she accompanied them through a vaulted foyer. Although the paintings, the chandelier and everything else wore dust covers, she couldn't fail to recognize the grandeur of the estate. She also couldn't fail to notice the long, curved banister of the magnificent spiral staircase.

It reminded her of the banister in Vanessa's house. But this one looked twice as long. Mallory suppressed a smile.

"Such a monster in mothballs, this house," Ellinor commented, glancing around. "I had a full staff of servants here before . . . Well, let's find the sherry, Third. Come, Miss Danner, to where my nephew and I really live." She led the way through a long side hall.

Mallory noted that the interior was magnificent. This monster was worthy of being whipped into shape by a butler and a well-trained, well-managed staff.

Ellinor went up a short stairway and opened a set of French doors into a small foyer. "Here we are. My apartment suite on the right. Third's quarters on the left. Privacy for the *grande dame* as well as the man about town."

West opened his door. "Let's settle in here."

"I'll just freshen up first," Ellinor called as she withdrew.

"Let me take your coat, Miss Danner," West said, settling both hands on Mallory's shoulders.

"That's one of a butler's opening lines," she replied teasingly. She slipped out of her gift from Vanessa, out from under West's more-than-helpful touch.

"You're the first female butler I've ever met, though I think I remember one in the news last year. What led you into a butlering career?"

"I apprenticed with my butler father, who apprenticed with his butler father, and so forth."

He shrugged out of his trench coat and hung it up. "My parents had a butler when I was a little brat. Good old Hyatt—he was ancient. I remember one of his daily duties was to iron the wrinkles out of the newspapers."

Mallory nodded. "I've done the same thing every morning for five years."

"Hyatt was a curmudgeon," West said, chuckling. "Especially toward bratty little boys like me. I did everything I could to torment him."

"Kids will be kids," Mallory reasoned, picturing West as a little rascal. He'd grown into such a big, handsome one.

West grinned. "Were you a devil of a kid? Or a perfect angel."

"An angel, of course." Being honest with him was out of the question; she'd been a mischievous child who'd often misbehaved. A familiar wave of guilt washed over her. Her mother's death had taught her a fast, cruel lesson and put a sudden, serious stop to her wild ways.

Mallory forced her mind back to the present. Either way, her childhood wasn't his concern.

"An angel, huh?" He eyed her speculatively for a moment, then said, "Come in and make yourself comfortable, Angel."

He motioned her in and she entered a living area that brought tropical islands to mind. Polynesian tapa cloth papered three walls. Rattan sofas and chairs were upholstered in batik print fabric. A wall of arched windows faced out to the Pacific Ocean.

Mallory walked over to take in the view and put a more comfortable distance between herself and West.

"What spectacular sunsets you must get," she marveled.

West shrugged. "I miss the majority of them. I travel a lot." He joined her at the window.

"For business or pleasure?"

"Both."

Mallory tried to recall ever hearing or reading that West Cade actually worked. His deep, golden tan suggested just the opposite. *HotScene* always referred to him as an "investor" and he certainly appeared to have invested every waking hour of his time on the sunniest playgrounds of the rich and famous: yachts, tennis courts, polo fields.

News photos always showed him in such locales, accompanied by a beautiful woman. A different one every time.

Mallory could feel his attention fix on her instead of out the window. He wasn't standing too close, but it felt that way. Too warm. Fighting the need to fan herself, she searched for something cool and distancing to say.

"Has your home base always been Pacific Heights, Mr. Cade?"

"Always," he replied. Then he suggested, "Let's both drop the formalities, okay? Call me 'West.'"

She nodded reluctantly, wishing for *more* formality to keep West at arm's length. "As a butler, I'm used to being called just 'Danner.'"

"I'd rather call you Angel," he murmured. "There's something heavenly about you. Your hair, maybe. Do you ever let it down?"

"It would only get in my way," she replied, although she pictured her hair loose and West running his fingers through it.

His green eyes teased her. "Aunt says you're single and unattached. As luck would have it, so am I."

"So I've heard on the news and read in the papers, West."

Mallory was trying hard to sound wry, doing her best to ignore West's sex appeal and remember that Ellinor had talked about offering her a job. If it panned out, working in a house where West Cade had bachelor's quarters would be a challenge. In that sense, flirting with him right now would be unwise. It would undermine her possible future here, not to mention her professionalism.

West said, "If the police chief doesn't keep his promise, you'll be reading about *yourself* in the papers. Did my aunt exaggerate about your black-belt tactics?"

"I just did what the situation required," Mallory replied, deciding she'd better start thinking and acting more like a butler. Modesty was an essential aspect of every good butler's manner, so she added, "Everything happened too fast to sort it out, Mr. Cade."

"'West.'"

Even his name was sexy, she thought as she observed his reflection on the windowpane. What a suave, self-assured rascal! His chestnut hair was tousled, his necktie somewhat askew, his shoulders broad, accented by his tailored suit.

Mallory edged a step away from him. He was too charismatic and masculine. And he had the knack of making her feel ultrafeminine, desirable, as if she had instantly become the center of his universe. West Cade hadn't gained and maintained a ladykiller reputation without having finely tuned instincts about the female psyche.

He cocked his head, studying her. "You know, you've got the most soothing voice I've ever heard."

"Butlers are trained to keep an even, modulated tone, West."

"Yours reminds me of a Polynesian massage, Angel."

"'Mallory,'" she corrected. She was surprised that she sounded calm, steady and reserved, for her knees felt wavery and her insides seemed to be dissolving. She wondered if a Polynesian massage felt as hedonistic—and arousing—as he made it sound.

West leaned one shoulder against the window and she caught his scent—all man. It stimulated her senses, causing chemical combustions, chain reactions, fantastic fantasies.

"'Mallory,'" he repeated, sounding rueful, as if she'd been cruel to deprive him of his pet name for her. "Who have you worked for, and where?"

"In Atherton, for Vanessa Canfield, who got married last month. She's now Lady Eaton. She was my first and only employer."

"Oh, Eaton," West said, nodding. "I saw an article about her wedding." His eyes snapped with a sudden light. "You're the pistol-packing butler she had. It's all coming back to me. You shot a loaded gun out of a jewel thief's hand. He was burgling Mrs. Canfield's safe."

Mallory shrugged and tried not to look too proud of the newspaper headlines she'd made last year. "Security was a minor part of my job. Much ado about nothing."

"Much ado about a lot. My compliments." He caught her hand and lifted it to his lips before she could react. Static electricity sparked between her fingers and his mouth.

"Oh!" She jumped at the sudden shock.

"Wow!" He pulled her closer. "Let's try that mouth to mouth."

"Don't let me stop you," Ellinor said from the door. "I do love a love scene."

Mallory jerked her hand away and whirled around. She heard West chuckle softly behind her. *Hot date*. He hadn't wasted a moment living up to his sizzling reputation!

"Your timing leaves a lot to be desired, Aunt Elli."

"Desire is the spice of life, Third. Pour some sherry for Miss Danner and me, please. None of your own pirate rum for us, thank you."

West guided Mallory to one of two facing sofas, then crossed the room to a small, built-in bar. He began uncorking a bottle.

"Angel and I are already on a first-name basis with each other, Aunt."

A pleased smile curved Ellinor's lips as she sank onto the sofa across from Mallory. "Well, then you should call me 'Elli,' Miss Danner."

"Oh, I couldn't, Mrs. Cade," Mallory protested.

"Why not? Because I'm an old woman who may be your employer? Don't let that worry you. What did you call Lady Eaton?"

Mallory frowned, unaware that she'd mentioned Vanessa in Ellinor's presence when the police had questioned everyone earlier.

"Did I say I worked for Lady Eaton?"

"Shame-shame, Aunt," West teased from the bar. "Were you listening at my keyhole again?"

"I was only waiting for an appropriate moment to enter, Third. I just happened to overhear the part about Lady Eaton." She focused on Mallory again, expectantly. "As you were saying . . ."

"I addressed her as 'Mrs. C.' when her name was Canfield," Mallory replied. "She always addressed me as 'Danner.'"

"Let's do the same then," Ellinor said. "I'll be your second Mrs. C., Danner."

Mallory hesitated, unsure how to respond to Ellinor's blithe assumption.

"I'm seeking a full-service position," Mallory said finally, hoping to clear up any misconception, "an entire household to manage, as I did before."

"I understand, Danner. I intend for my enormous house to become a hub of society again. Before I die, I want to live for a while as I once did."

Looking perplexed at his aunt's statements, West served the sherries, then sat beside Mallory with his rum.

"I don't understand, Aunt. After all these years of seclusion?"

"Third, I know this is all terribly sudden. I'll explain later about the new antidepressant I've begun taking. Right now, let's drink a toast to Danner—my savior— and my new butler, if she wants the job."

Shrugging, West turned his attention to Mallory. He tipped his glass in a symbolic gesture, chorusing with Elli, "To Danner."

He sampled his rum and glanced at Mallory next to him. If she came to work for his aunt, she'd be present twenty-four hours a day. A glowing prospect, since he traveled a lot and disliked leaving Aunt all alone.

He also couldn't forget the spark of electricity; his lips still tingled from kissing Mallory's hand. At the same time, though, he asked himself whether a female butler's presence would put a crimp in his life-style. Would she purse her lips when she toured the house and saw his mirrored bedroom ceiling? Would she turn up her nose at the silk robes and kimonos he kept stocked in his closet for female companions? Would she be amused by his escapades, or tolerant of them? Maybe she'd just ignore his high jinks, the way Aunt did.

"What do you think, Third?"

"I don't know," West replied. "Having a butler and doing the house up will be a huge change for you. Are you sure you feel up to it?"

"Oh, yes! This new medicine I mentioned—" Elli broke off and looked at Mallory. "If you accept my offer, we'll be working closely together. You shouldn't accept without knowing that my doctor is treating me for depression. For years, and for very personal reasons, I refused to take any medication. I haven't been chipper or eager to socialize until now."

"Thank you for telling me," Mallory said. "I wanted to ask, but didn't know how."

Elli nodded, smiling. "I don't blame you. It's common knowledge that I've been a recluse, and natural for you to wonder why. I haven't had servants for ages—except for Michelle, a personal maid who was here a short while over a year ago after I had a small stroke."

"She was nice," West put in, "a big help to Aunt."

"Yes," Elli agreed, then continued explaining. "She quit abruptly without notice after a few months." She glanced at West and raised an eyebrow. "I thought she looked rather pregnant at the time she left."

West's head jerked back. "So? I had nothing to do with it, if that's what you're hinting."

"I didn't hint a thing," Elli said mildly.

West hunched his shoulders. "She must have had a boyfriend we didn't know about."

"Must have," Elli agreed, without sounding convinced. "She was a very private person."

West saw Mallory glance at him with suspicion—and disapproval. He rattled the ice in his glass, mentally raising his defenses. Her expression made him think she might run a prim, prissy ship if she became Aunt's butler. He'd much rather come and go without anyone disapproving of him and his activities at every turn.

If she did, she'd learn that he came and went as he damn well pleased. Not that he'd been living it up that much recently at home or overseas. Either these were sobering times or maturity was creeping up on him, as his aunt kept predicting it would.

Whatever the case, he didn't have to like or conform to the new conservatism. Damned if his midthirties, or the prevailing moral climate, would slow him down until he was ready. Warren Beatty had played the open field until his midfifties before settling down. West couldn't see himself doing anything less.

"Third, what are you frowning about?"

West came back to himself with a start. "I just hope you aren't jumping the gun, Aunt. I've never seen you so optimistic and outgoing."

"A medical miracle," said Elli. "You know, this house was once an outstanding setting for charity benefits and social gatherings, and I was once quite the hostess. I can do much good as my old self, back in the thick of things."

Mallory couldn't help feeling inspired by the possibilities Mrs. C. had conjured up as she'd spoken. What a place this would be to whip into shape! She knew just how she'd spearhead a renovation, interview and hire a staff, inventory the linens and china and silver, oversee every detail.

"What do you say, Danner? I'll match your present salary and raise it by fifteen percent."

Mallory sipped her sherry and tried to think. *Fifteen percent!* The challenging position and generous terms were more than tempting, especially if West spent most of his time elsewhere. He must, since he couldn't have gotten his tropic-tone tan in cool, foggy San Francisco.

If life was a beach for him, all the better. His roguish appeal and rakish charm wouldn't be easy to ignore. As butler, she'd have to steer clear of involvement with him. He had already electrocuted her hand with an idle kiss.

"Would I be serving both you and West, Mrs. C.?"

"West isn't home that often. But let's agree on a *twenty* percent increase, since he'll be here once in a while. Won't you, Third?"

"Once in a while . . ." he confirmed distractedly, rattling his ice again.

That sounded infrequent enough, Mallory thought. All the better if his unfocused, faraway expression meant he was picturing his imminent return to the tanning circuit.

"In that case," she found herself saying, "I can start at the end of next week, when escrow closes on Lady Eaton's house." She'd just be sure to keep that "rather pregnant" maid in mind twenty-four hours a day.

Ellinor's blue eyes sparkled. "You'll do it? Be my *aide de camp*—and guardian angel, if necesssary?"

"Yes, ma'am. But I think we should begin on a trial basis to prevent any misunderstanding if it turns out we're not right for each other."

"Thirty days, then," Ellinor declared. "I'll warn you, I need some social and cultural re-education. I'm years behind the times."

Excited to be employed again, Mallory replied, "We'll take everything step by step."

"Done!" Elli patted West's hand. "Don't frown and worry about me. Danner is just the assistant I need."

West assumed a benign smile that masked more than his concern for her. Although Mallory seemed to be a godsend for Aunt, what if she turned out to be a pain in the groin for him? Her dignified reserve might be warning that her rules and regs for the house would reflect her demeanor. No this. No that. No naughty nonsense.

Well, so what? He lived by his own lights, not anyone else's. By accepting this job she'd have to accept the consequences. He wasn't going to ignore that she was beautiful, desirable and interesting. In fact, he'd like to get to know her much, much better. Something tucked way away in her eyes and her smile gave his male intuition the idea that she had a saucy, sexy, sizzling side.

If his intuition was right, and she kept a devilish streak under wraps, he wanted to unwrap it. She might have rules and regs, but so did he.

Rule number one from now on: Tempt the devil in Danner.

"Propose a toast, Third."

West turned a roguish smile on Mallory and touched his glass to hers. "May sparks strike again, Angel."

3

MALLORY SPENT her final days at the gatehouse assuring herself that she hadn't made a bad decision in agreeing to work for Ellinor Cade. She had phoned her father, and Dad had expressed strong reservations about West.

Meanwhile, the news media reported nothing of the incident in the alley. The police chief apparently kept mum. At times, Mallory half expected Ellinor to phone and say she'd changed her mind about returning to society.

No such call came, but an employment contract from Ellinor arrived in the mail. Mallory signed it and mailed it back to Pacific Heights with her résumé. Overnight, she received written confirmation of employment.

The day before the new owners were to take possession of Vanessa's estate, Mallory began packing up her belongings. There wasn't much. Clothing. Books. Family photographs of her parents and triplet sisters. She lingered over the photos, spreading them out on the coffee table, remembering—

The phone rang. It was her father, still sounding troubled. "Lory, I wish you'd reconsider about working for Mrs. Cade. Her nephew's reputation is far from sterling. As a young, attractive woman, you'll be at a professional disadvantage."

"Dad, I'm certain I can work there without inviting any passes from Mr. Cade. I handled Vanessa's son without any trouble." She hedged the main issue, adding, "Anyway, West Cade isn't my type."

"The tabloids say he's every woman's type," her father complained. "Your sisters agree, I might add."

"I know, Dad. They phoned yesterday after you told them where I'd be working." They had also squealed, sighed, and swooned over the subject of West Cade.

Dad warned, "Keep up your guard. Don't forget anything I've taught you." He started a pop-quiz on the cardinal rules of butlering. "Who sets the standard of good manners and good taste in a household?"

"The butler, Dad."

"How does she draw and hold the professional line?"

"By being friendly, but *never* familiar."

"Three good words that describe a perfect butler?"

"Proper, stiff and inscrutable."

"What opinions may a butler offer?"

"Only requested ones." She ticked off several more answers without the questions. "A butler's bow is always respectful, never servile. Her social circle can't be the same as her employer's. She lives a separate life. Evenhanded with everyone. Never haughty and aloof. Always civil and low-key."

"Always," he agreed. "Will you keep everything in mind? For dear old Dad's peace of mind?"

"I won't forget a thing," she assured him.

"Well," he said hesitantly, "goodbye, then, for now. Watch your step with that swinging single."

"'Bye, Dad." He was hopelessly, endearingly old school and old-fashioned. "Don't worry."

She hung up and was turning back to the family photos, when the phone rang again. It was that swinging single.

"I'm passing through Atherton right now," he said. "Need help moving, Angel?"

Mallory's heart began beating faster. "Not really. I have relatively few belongings." She'd love to have him help her, but she had to behave like his aunt's employee, not herself.

"I'll lend a hand, anyway. I'm driving a van and I'll bring us some lunch."

"I really don't need help, Mr. Cade."

"'West,'" he corrected. "It's not one of the four-letter words nice butlers don't use." His tone changed, took a seductive turn. "Is your heavenly hair clipped back in that barrette right now?"

"Always." Mallory combed her fingers through her freshly shampooed curls and waves. Her hair was drying naturally, but West didn't have to know it was having its own way at the moment. It would only give him creative ideas—like the ones she'd been having about him all week.

She wouldn't want him to think she was thrilled by his call, even though her heart had begun pounding the moment she'd realized it was him. His voice was so deep and seductive over the phone, but letting him know it would be playing right into his hands. He'd have them all over her if she didn't set the right tone, right from the start.

"Angel, you need some serious loosening up."

Mallory could just imagine how he'd go about doing it. He would be a skilled lover. Even so, she should politely ignore his statement, according to the rules, so she would.

She said, "Why aren't you out of town like you said you'd be?"

"I'll tell you over lunch. You're at 210 Sylvan Drive, right?"

"Yes, but—"

"I'll be there in a flash." He hung up.

Mallory stared at the receiver in her hand. West had more self-confidence than any man should rightly have. Good thing he didn't know he'd played a starring role in her thoughts, dreams and sexual fantasies for almost a week now.

She left the phone and went in search of her barrette. It wasn't in the kitchen or bedroom or bathroom. She cursed under her breath and made a face at herself in the mirror. Less than three minutes after she'd hung up the phone, the intercom connection to the gate buzzed.

Mallory punched the intercom button, hoping that the gardener would be out there. "May I help you?"

"Lunch is served," West announced.

She looked through the window blinds at the sleek minivan stopped at the gate. "You said a flash, West, not a fraction of one."

He chuckled smugly. "Aren't car phones a big time-saver? Let me in before the champagne gets warm."

"May I first point out that you have no valid reason to be here?" she said, making an all-out effort to sound proper, stiff and inscrutable, instead of excited.

"As Aunt Elli's nephew, I've got every reason to verify your credentials before you move into the house I live in with her."

Mallory ran a hand through her hair and down the front of the gray sweatshirt she was wearing with matching sweatpants. "I'm not dressed for a job interview."

"Neither am I. I'm a live-in-the-moment guy, so sue me. After lunch."

Mallory threw the gate switch. She smoothed her sweats and slipped her bare feet into a pair of thong sandals.

It took West just a few seconds to park, unload a wicker picnic hamper and appear at the door of the small, stone gatehouse. He was wearing loose gray sweats like hers, and worn sneakers.

"Well, aren't we twins," he noted, flashing an amused grin when she opened the door and let him in.

She observed that his hair was as tousled as it had been before, his eyes just as teasing and green. No doubt he'd be *People* magazine's next Sexiest Man Alive. That week's issue would sell out overnight. She'd buy one for sure.

"Come in," she said, "and please excuse the disorder. I'm packing to move."

"You look just like I pictured you," he said, "with your hair doing its own thing."

"Such a mess." She waved one hand at the untidy room and strove to look friendly, but *never* familiar.

He immediately spied the photos on the coffee table. "Anyone I know?"

"My family."

"Well, I know one of them—you." He stepped closer to the table. "Mind if I look?"

"Not if you're interested." Courtesy and diplomacy were essential butler traits, she reminded herself. Being the quintessential butler around West was a prime necessity. Especially right now.

He studied the pictures for a moment and picked one up to examine more closely. "Am I seeing triple?"

Mallory nodded. "My triplet sisters. Deirdre, Dana and Dawn were two years old then." She pointed herself out. "Me, age thirteen. And my father."

She was glad that she'd already packed away the snapshots of two boyfriends she'd had at different times in the past. Kent and Clark had been serious men who'd kept their noses to the grindstone. Kent had been Vanessa's accountant. Clark had been a computer consultant. Lovemaking hadn't been a high point with either of them.

One look at their sober expressions would have told West more than he had any business knowing about the involvements she'd had. His quick wit would probably combine their names into Clark Kent—two nerds in one.

He picked up a snapshot that showed Mallory wearing a kitchen apron and cradling Dana in her arms. "You look like the chief cook and bottlewasher."

"I was. My mother died of cancer when I was twelve."

"I'm sorry. My own mother died last year of the same thing." He looked up at Mallory, his expression more serious and reflective than she'd seen it so far. "Twelve was pretty young to step into your mom's shoes. You're still taking care of people, aren't you?"

Mallory glanced away, thinking of the high-school football games, dances and proms she had missed, the dates and carefree teenage fun she'd rarely had.

She replied without answering his question. "My sisters are coeds at the same Arizona college now. Dad remarried and then retired to Tucson to be close to them. I help them pay their school tuition as much as I can."

His intent gaze probed. "Who helps *you*, Angel?"

"I'm self-sufficient as long as I'm employed."

He picked up another picture that showed her, age sixteen, reading from a book to her sisters at bedtime. The title of the book had photographed clearly and he read it out loud: "*Fairy Tales Around the World.*"

"The girls loved them," she said.

His eyes probed deeper than before. "Did you?"

She nodded. There was no reason to keep it a secret. But she looked away again, guarding the secret that deep in her heart she was a romantic, though not one who always believed in happily ever after. Not always, just every once in a rare while . . .

To her relief, he changed his focus and also the subject, asking, "What do you wear when you work? I remember Hyatt wore a tuxedo and bow-tie."

"A simple business suit. Set your basket down while I clear the table."

He shook his head. "Leave everything. I brought a fully equipped picnic, Angel, not a sit-down lunch. Let's eat outside."

"I suppose we could," Mallory reluctantly agreed, wishing for a higher degree of formality to hold him at arm's length. "There's a lawn area and duck pond behind the main house. No ducks in residence, though."

He smiled. "I'll quack for atmosphere. Let's soak up some rays."

Mallory showed him outside, up the front walkway of Vanessa's imposing Tudor-style house, around to the lush, green lawn and stone-bordered pond in back.

"Pacific Heights seems cramped compared with this," West commented as they both settled on the grass, in the sunshine. "Homeowners get more real estate for the money here."

"Yes, but gardening costs are higher."

Mallory watched him open the hamper and lift out a bottle of champagne, herbed breadsticks, dilled salmon, a small raspberry cheesecake in the shape of a heart. A lover's lunch. Courtesy of lover boy, himself. Too bad she couldn't cut loose and thoroughly enjoy it with him. What an experience *that* would be!

West brought out two plastic champagne flutes, then popped the cork from the bottle into the pond. He filled both flutes and lounged back on one elbow. "Drink up. Relax."

Mallory sipped the champagne sparingly. Too much might lower her guard. It wouldn't be smart to let it down close to a hot date like West Cade. He'd think nothing of taking full advantage to the fullest extent. She visualized him taking ravishing advantage of her, then glanced over and found him looking disgruntled.

"You're not enjoying my little surprise," he said. "You've read all about my . . . adventures, and now you think I dropped by to have a naked lunch with you instead of a simple picnic."

Mallory admitted, "I have reservations about you, and good reasons for having them."

"If you're referring to my freestyle life-style, Angel, I make no apologies for it. And I don't impose it on anyone else."

"I'm referring to Vanessa's youngest son," she explained. "He took an inappropriate interest in me when I began here as butler, and—"

"I don't blame him," West cut in.

"Thank you, but the point is that Vanessa and I had to put him firmly in his place. I'd be ignoring past experience not to suspect you and this seductive lunch you brought with you."

"Next time I'll bring cheeseburgers and root beer, okay?" he offered. "I'm here out of concern for my vulnerable Aunt Elli. To make sure you're everything you've seemed to be."

"Aren't my résumé and references proof enough?"

He shook his head. "They didn't include a description of Lady Eaton's estate. I was curious about the size and scope of the house you've been managing, how you've been living."

"The champagne and heart-shaped cheesecake just happened along for the ride?" she queried with a small smile. He was making a persuasive case for his visit, on the surface at least. She was even getting persuaded, beneath the surface.

He countered, "What I brought is appropriate for Valentine's Day. Happy February 14."

She blinked. "Is it? I'd forgotten."

"This was the only ready-to-go picnic the gourmet grocery store was offering today, Angel. Stop looking suspicious of me and my motives."

Mallory felt her guard slip several notches. To crank it up, she renewed her formal tone and told him, "'Angel' is too familiar a form of address, West. Especially since I'm your aunt's butler."

"You aren't on her payroll yet." He handed her a plate of salmon. "Lemon with this? Tartar sauce?"

"No, thank you. It looks delicious, as is."

"You look the same, Angel, as is." He broke into a grin worthy of the naughtiest rascal.

She couldn't help but grin back at him and only half-seriously warn, "You're making me suspect your motives again, West."

"Eat up," he said. "I'll behave." He served himself, then kept his word by asking impersonal, businesslike questions about her butlering style and skills. Mallory began relaxing, enjoying the lunch, the sunshine and West. He was a witty, natural tease who joked and laughed easily. He showed a more serious side, however, when he spoke about his mother's death the year before, and his father's death many years ago.

"I'm the last male Cade," he said after the cheesecake was just a sweet memory. Stretching out on his back, he clasped his hands behind his head and sighed. "If I don't sire heirs and heiresses someday, I'm the end of a line."

Mallory gazed out over the pond and mused, "Most people marry at some point, have a family."

"What about you?" he asked. "Or are you dedicated to being a professional caretaker?"

She'd never thought of herself that way... not before he'd put it that way. It set her on the defensive and she coolly replied, "I've been happy in my work. Happier than I think I'd be with a husband right now."

"What about having kids?"

"I've already mothered three children."

"You mean your sisters." He turned another probing gaze on her.

"Yes." Mallory looked away and toyed with a blade of grass to avoid his scrutiny. She'd never found it easy to sort out or express her doubts and conflicts about having children. "They were a lot of hard work."

"And no play?" West rejoined.

Unwilling to show that he'd hit the mark, she shrugged. "When I'm ready to settle down with someone, I suppose I will."

"With what sort of man?"

"A dependable, hardworking, serious-minded person," she replied in a challenging tone, prepared for him to scoff. To his credit, he only asked another question.

"In the meantime, where do you meet people to date and have fun with?"

She raised her eyebrows, and more of her defenses. "Oh, here and there, now and then." He didn't have to know that she hadn't dated anyone since Kent last year. "As for fun... it's not my main goal in life."

"It's mine." He gazed up at the sky. "I love to play, live it up and hang loose. Call me irresponsible. Everyone else does, even Aunt Elli."

Irresponsible, Mallory complied silently. For that reason alone, she should have a more negative opinion of him than what she had managed to form so far. He was a happy-go-lucky playboy, fooling around, putting a few smooth moves on his aunt's new butler. He seemed to have no responsibilities and nothing else to do. Not a care in the world.

As a purposeful, productive, dutiful member of society, she should be put off by his shortcomings. Maybe it was just his sincere concern for his aunt that she found so appealing. She hoped so.

West blew a sigh to the sky. "What's irresponsible about letting the good times roll and rolling right along with them?"

As he spoke, a pair of mallards flew over the pond and settled onto the still water. They began quacking and splashing around together and Mallory was startled to realize they were mating.

"What's the commotion?" West asked, lifting his head to view the pond.

Mallory began stacking plates. "Valentine's Day," she murmured, feeling her face warm in response to the drake's and hen's amorous, ecstatic cries.

"My kind of fun," West observed with uninhibited interest. He sat up to see better. "Imagine *us* being that up-front about our own lusty, passionate drives and desires."

Mallory went right ahead and imagined it in lusty, passionate, vivid detail. Then, eager to escape the evocative sex scene, she pushed up her sweatshirt sleeves and began packing the lunch things into the basket.

"Hey, that's *my* job as host, Angel." He clasped her wrist to stop her. "I can't seem to quit calling you that, can I?"

West saw Mallory's cheeks tint a deep pink as she focused on his hand. He slid his fingers up to the cuff at her elbow, stroking her skin, so pale and soft. He could faintly see her nipples peaking against her sweatshirt, and a tiny pulse leaping in the hollow of her throat.

Oh, she was right to suspect him of wanting to seduce her. He wanted to kiss her luscious lips and locate every one of her hot spots. Her proper manner and perfect manners made him itch to trip her mainspring.

He gazed deep into her eyes, whispered, "Do you kiss on the first date, Mallory?"

She focused on his lips. "Never."

"On the second?"

"Rarely." She heard her voice tremble, felt her arm quiver as his hand curled around it. He was the most charismatic, provocative man, and she couldn't help wondering how it would feel to kiss him.

"Where do you find the patience to wait?"

"I . . ." Mallory felt an urge to lean toward him as he leaned closer. She warned herself that a kiss would be a big mistake, but an impulsive inner voice urged her on. *Do it! Cut loose!*

She struggled against giving in to temptation. Now was no time for one of her unexpected impulses to pop out.

"You're beautiful," West murmured. "Your skin . . . your hair . . . your everything . . ."

Time seemed to have stopped. The air felt warm, heavy and moist. She felt his fingertips tracing sensational circles on her inner arm, making her heart beat faster. He leaned closer, angled his head. A moment more and his lips would touch hers. His chest would rub up against her breasts.

Just in time, she pulled away and stood. Her head spun, her knees shook, and the voice of temptation mercifully shut up.

"Thank you for lunch, West."

West blinked momentarily, then slowly grinned. "It was my pleasure, Mallory. See? I can get your name right if I try really hard."

"Keep trying," she said with an encouraging nod, relieved to see him look somewhat dizzy himself as he rose to his feet beside her.

Walking back to the gatehouse, West commented, "The résumé you sent was interesting. You're licensed to pilot small planes and even helicopters."

"Yes. My flight ratings are current. Will Mrs. C. need a pilot?"

"No, but I might need one myself, depending on circumstances. I do a lot of island hopping. So much that I've thought about buying my own aircraft and hiring a full-time pilot. If I do, maybe you could fill in on the regular's time off."

Spare no expense to maintain that islander suntan, Mallory mentally teased him. She visualized him lounging on coral sands, kissed by the sun. The image transformed into one of him tanning nude and it stuck in her mind, much as the sight of the ducks had imprinted its own erotic stamp.

She could hear them quacking again, churning up the pond with zeal, reminding her of the romance and sexual passion that were missing in her own life. West's touch had promised splendor in the grass . . . his tantalizing lips had almost . . .

"Did you soak up too much sun during lunch, or are you blushing, Mallory?"

Her breath caught. West was too observant. She drew on five years of professional poise to form a reply.

"I burn easily. It must be the sun."

"You turned hot pink when our feathered friends started having fun. Arousing, wasn't it?"

She frowned, determined to divert him from what seemed to be his favorite topic: sex. It was becoming hers, too. She forced herself to block out his everpresent sex appeal. "You were talking about island hopping and pilots."

"If you insist. Would you mind taking the controls occasionally?"

"Mrs. C. would have to approve."

"She will."

"Would I be prying to ask why she became so reclusive?"

He slowed as they approached her door. "No, but she'd probably rather tell you herself, in her own time." He glanced back at the big house. "City living will be a change for you after this."

"Yes, I'll miss Atherton. I've enjoyed living here, but all good things come to an end."

"Who says they do, Angel?" Realizing his slip, he snapped his fingers. "There I go again."

"You caught your mistake this time so you're forgiven."

"Thanks." He stood on her doorstep, looking down at her as if lunch hadn't satisfied his appetite. "To keep our own good thing going, what can I do to help you move?"

"Nothing. Really. Two trips in my car will do it."

"One in my van would do it fast and easy."

"I'm not all packed yet."

"Call me when you are."

Determined to resist, she said, "You must have better uses for your time, West."

"There are no demands on my time for the rest of the day. I've had to keep a constant eye on Aunt Elli but this afternoon she's safe at home, playing canasta with her doctor. Besides, the sooner you're moved in, the sooner I fly out again."

"To where?"

"A Polynesian archipelago. You should see it— beautiful, pristine beaches on every island. One of my own favorite islands is ripe for sale right now and I'm ripe to sell it."

"An island of your own?" An almost staggering thought.

"No. I sold the last one I owned to one of my clients."

"Clients in what sense?"

"In the sense that I work for myself, selling islands around the world to clients who want to buy them."

Unsteadied to learn that life was more than a full-time playground for West Cade, she rocked back on her heels.

"Surprised, Angel?"

She couldn't conceal it, although a butler really shouldn't look shocked, rocked or taken off-guard except in dire circumstances. Earthquakes. Hurricanes. Tornadoes. Avalanches.

"What's so surprising about my work?" he asked.

"What isn't?" she countered. "The press always describe you as an investor, which often means . . . well, rich and idle."

"Unfortunately the reporters focus on my leisure time and nothing else," he said. "But then, I've worked for only a couple of years. Before that, I was just what you said, 'rich and idle.' I spent my time making my so-called reputation for appreciation. You don't think much of it, do you?"

"I don't think of it much, West." She was deliberately being oblique because a butler who knew of her employer's nephew's indiscretions shouldn't speak of them to anyone—not even to the nephew.

Shifting the conversation back to neutral territory, she commented, "Selling islands is unusual work."

"You dodge every leading question I ask, Angel. Are you a prude or just sound a lot like one?"

"*Very* unusual work," she persisted, to make him decide she was a prude, too priggish to even answer his question. Better than his thinking she was a hot prospect.

"Unusual enough," he finally agreed, giving her a slow, savvy, sidelong smile. "And lots of fun. You'll have to fly me on a sales trip sometime and see for yourself . . . won't you?"

4

MALLORY MOVED to San Francisco without accepting West's offers to help her move. Maddeningly persistent, he had phoned her after lunch and offered again. Then phoned that same evening. Then again the next morning. Each time she had withstood his charming attempts to change her mind.

When she drove up to the door of Ellinor's Pacific Heights mansion, he was Johnny-on-the-doorstep to lend her a hand. She couldn't deter him on his own turf.

He had the upper hand, saying, "No, I'll carry it all upstairs, not you. I'm the muscleman for this job, Angel."

As if she hadn't noticed every manly muscle.

Elli came out to greet her. "Come with me, Danner. I'll show you more of the house, and your quarters."

She led the way inside through a vast, Spanish-tiled kitchen equipped with a walk-in refrigerator and a stained-glass skylight.

"Third and I cook up our own meals together in here when he's not entertaining one of his lady companions." She paused in midstep, looked thoughtful. "Although he hasn't had any recently that I know of. Slowing down as men do, I suppose."

She glanced at Mallory and added, "He tells me he brought lunch to you yesterday."

"It was very kind of him," Mallory murmured uncomfortably.

At that moment, West came through the kitchen, hefting two of her boxes, making it look like child's play. He wore sweats again, streamlined hunter green ones that accented his eyes and his muscular build.

Mallory tried not to notice. The less she noticed, the sooner she'd stop feeling hot, bothered and flustered about this man.

"Come," said Elli, and moved through the kitchen to a long hallway lined with closed doors. "These are the housekeeper's, cooks' and maids' rooms." She opened one door. "This was Michelle's when she was here."

Mallory glanced into the room, recalling Elli's speculation that Michelle had been pregnant. Had West had his way with the young housemaid right here—or in his own bed? Had his indignant denial last week been a smoke screen to hide the truth?

Mallory was acutely conscious of West close behind her. She was dressed in a tailored gray suit, a bow-tie blouse and low heels. Lover boy should be getting the message—all work, no play, prude, prude, prude.

"Here we are," Elli said, turning another corner and then opening a door. "Butler's quarters."

Mallory entered a small suite of rooms decorated in sea blue and beige. The sitting room had its own little fireplace flanked by bookshelves. There was a wallpapered bedroom with a four-poster bed, a roomy closet and tiled bath, a pantry nook with a hot plate and a microwave oven.

"Thank you," she said to Elli. "It's so pretty." Even nicer than her former quarters in Atherton. "More space than I really need."

"Enjoy, Danner."

West set the two boxes on the bed and came out of the bedroom rubbing his hands together. "I had a brand-new mattress put in for you, Angel." He paused for maximum effect. "A virgin."

Watching her eyes flash a spirited reproof at him, West hid a smile. He wasn't deterred. The devil in Danner couldn't hide forever, not from the devil in him.

"THIRD," Elli said at breakfast a week and a half after Mallory had taken charge, "what happened to your trip?"

West shrugged and stirred his coffee. "Something came up, so I postponed it, I guess. Whatever."

"Have you decided about buying your own plane yet?"

"Not yet. Still mulling it over."

He sat back in his chair at the breakfast table and basked in the sunlight streaming through the freshly washed windows of the morning room. Mallory had rounded up a regiment of window washers and put them to work the day she arrived. Since then she hadn't been idle one minute.

"Something came up, such as . . . ?" Elli raised her eyebrows at him.

"Your new medicine," West hedged. "I don't want to be halfway around the world if the pills stop working."

"And don't want to be far from Danner, either," his aunt noted.

He didn't lie and deny it. He just scowled. "I don't like the way your new cook and his assistant leer at Angel."

"They don't leer," Elli objected. "They're just two young, handsome Hungarians—" she paused, looking amused "—or should I say, Hunkarians—who are very pleased to be working under Danner's supervision again."

"Too damned pleased," he muttered.

Elli waved his grumbles off. "I'm glad she was able to retrieve some of Lady Eaton's former staff and put them to work here for me. You know, they actually quit the new jobs they'd gotten, preferring to work with her."

West found himself wishing that the two bachelor cooks were eunuchs. Better that than hunks with flashing white smiles and smoldering dark eyes. They burned for Mallory; he was sure of it.

So he had postponed his trip, day by day. Instead of flying to the South Pacific, selling an island and frolicking in Papeete with a Tahitian hula dancer, he'd stuck around the house to keep a vigilant eye on Mallory. One outright leer and he'd fire both cooks on the spot.

Elli was studying him with interest. "I've never seen you look jealous before, Third."

"I'm naturally green-eyed, Aunt," he said, fending her off by winking at her.

She nodded, looking smug about his reply rather than fooled by it. "I had hoped you'd delay your trip.

Now that you have, I hope you're beginning to see something missing in your easy-come, easy-go lifestyle. Among other things, structure, stability and meaning come to mind."

"Not to *my* mind, Aunt." He quickly changed the subject. "You're the picture of health and high spirits this morning. Medicine's still working?"

Elli breathed a happy, contented sigh. "Last week I was a recluse. Today I'm a *grande dame* with a butler, a housekeeper, two cooks and three housemaids."

A plump, matronly, Teutonic housekeeper named Berthe, West grumbled silently. *Three stout, hearty, over-fifty housemaids named Rosa, Edith and Pearl.* Nothing pert and pretty to divert his eye from the beautiful butler who wouldn't give him the time of day.

All around him, the house was taking sudden shape under Mallory's expert direction. A small army of painters was busy right now laying drop cloths and erecting ladders in the library and the drawing room. West could smell the paint. He could hear Mallory's calm, modulated voice giving final instructions to the captain of the crew.

"Every paint spill must be cleaned up without a trace," she was saying with unquestionable authority. "No specks and spatters anywhere, please."

"None anywhere, ma'am," West heard the man assure her.

He wondered if the guy had already taken note of the butler's shapely legs, shrouded though they were by the midiskirt of her beige business suit. A leg man wouldn't miss her slim, pretty ankles. Right at this moment he was probably licking his lips at the sight of them. Damn him!

Hearing Mallory's footsteps turn toward the morning room, West frowned at his orange juice. Moodiness wasn't his style, but he was out of sorts now. He hadn't been able to catch her alone, day or night, since she'd moved in. There had hardly been a minute to tease or tempt or dare the devil in her.

She'd been surrounded by other men—cooks, window washers, rug cleaners, and now the paint squad. She'd spent the rest of the time conferring with Aunt about one thing or another. She had spent one of her days off at karate practice, the other one flying a plane. He had tried to invite himself along and gotten nowhere. He looked up and hid his frustration behind a teasing grin as Mallory came through the door.

"Good morning, sunshine." He rose from his chair. "Sleep well on virgin territory?"

Mallory nodded. "Yes, thank you. Please don't stand."

"Aunt Elli would spank me if I didn't, Angel." He continued standing. "She taught me the better half of my manners while I was growing up."

"Have a seat with us, Danner," Elli invited, pouring coffee from a silver pot into an extra cup for her. "You and I have to take a few moments and plan a shopping trip for this afternoon."

Mallory hesitated, faced with a dilemma. As a rule, butlers didn't join in at the table. But if West was going to remain standing there in skintight, black bike shorts, she knew she'd better sit down so he'd sit down. A moment more and it would become obvious she was staring.

Paired with a black tank top, his shorts hugged his slim waist, narrow hips, muscled thighs, and showcased the sex appeal of everything in between. The sooner he lowered into his chair, the better for the butler.

She settled across the table from him, took a sip of coffee and asked the sort of polite, obvious question a butler was supposed to ask. "Taking a bike ride today, West?"

"Up and down hill and dale," he confirmed as he sat down. "Gotta keep in shape."

Any better shape, she thought, and she'd have buckled at the knees when he'd stood up. She turned to Ellinor.

"Before I forget, Mrs. C., the ballroom floor should be sanded and varnished for the dancing at the ball."

"Arrange it, then," Elli agreed. "It's so exciting to plan a masquerade ball, my second debut before San Francisco society. I'm making a list of invitations. One hundred guests and still counting."

Feeling West's eyes seek hers across the table, Mallory avoided them. "You mentioned before that you wanted to do some shopping, Mrs. C.?"

"Yes. I want to be decked out in style again from hats to high heels. Are both in vogue right now?"

"Both," Mallory confirmed, hopeful that West would be bored by a fashion report and leave. Or at least turn his attention back to his orange juice and stop making the butler feel like the tastiest thing at the table.

"Feathered evening hats are making a comeback," she informed Elli, "and heels of every height are featured in the spring collections."

Keeping abreast of current fashion and style was a vital part of being a butler. Knowing the finest wines, the best restaurants, the who's who on the social scene were all part of the job.

"Hemlines are going thigh-high," West put in, giving Mallory a roguish eye, "even on butler suits."

"Not according to my butler manual," Mallory smoothly replied. Knowing just where to shop, she started listing a few of the best places aloud for Elli. "We can go to Saks, I. Magnin, Neiman Marcus. Downtown would be best for a start."

Elli's eyes sparkled with anticipation. "Yes, we'll circle Union Square and pop into old, faithful Gump's, too." She glanced at her watch. "Let's be ready to go at two p.m. sharp. Third, may we drive your two-seater downtown for fun?"

"All yours, ladies," West said.

"Would you mind driving, Danner?"

"Not at all, Mrs. C." Mallory imagined that the driver's seat would still be red-hot from the last time West had occupied it. An eyeful of him in his bike shorts would fire any female's imagination, butler or not.

MALLORY TOOK a high-tea shopping break with Ellinor in the glass-domed Garden Court restaurant of the Palace Hotel. A chamber quartet played selections from Bach and Vivaldi. Elli was in a reminiscent mood.

"Once upon a time, years and years ago," she recalled, her eyes dreamy with memories, "I got my second proposal of marriage in this very same restaurant. I was a young widow . . ."

Mallory bit into a cucumber sandwich, eager for Elli to go on about what had happened once upon a time. It was sounding like a real-life fairy tale. Mallory was dying to hear it.

"My husband, Charles, had died in a flu epidemic," Elli continued. "It wasn't long before Wynston Packard asked me to marry him. Poor Wyn was crazy about me, but I . . ."

Mallory was hanging on every word, picturing Elli's suitor on one knee asking Elli to marry him.

Dreamily Elli went on, "I suppose I should be ashamed to say so, but I couldn't say yes to Wyn because I was desperately in love with someone else."

Mallory had inched forward in her chair. She held her breath in anticipation of what Elli would say next. But then Elli's blue eyes began clouding, so Mallory refreshed the tea in Elli's cup and offered her more milk and sugar.

"Sugar to sweeten my bittersweet frame of mind, Danner?"

"No need to upset yourself for no reason, Mrs. C. You're still recovering from a long illness, after all."

Elli nodded thoughtfully and sipped her tea. Then she set down the cup and inquired, "Have you ever been in love with another woman's husband?"

"No." Tact and sympathy prompted Mallory to add, "Not so far, anyway."

"Well, I have, Danner. The love of my life was Wynston's best friend, married to a woman more attracted to his fortune than to him. It was true love at first sight for Sebastian and me. We did our best to resist temptation, but our social circles overlapped and brought us together all the time."

Elli stopped to stir sugar into her tea. "Sebastian wanted a divorce, and requested one several times, but Ophelia refused to give him one. You see the dilemma we faced."

Mallory nodded sympathetically, inferring from Elli's expression that there had been no fairy-tale ending to her love story.

Elli sighed. "Our love was everything I'd never experienced in my short marriage—so desperate, overwhelming and passionate. When I became pregnant, I told no one, not even Sebastian."

Eyes downcast, Elli paused to collect herself. "I miscarried in the third month upon receiving word that Sebastian had been killed in an automobile accident. It was more than I could take and I suffered a nervous breakdown. That began my long depression. I secluded myself with precious memories for years, and refused medication until recently."

"I'm so sorry, Mrs. C." Mallory felt emotion lump in her throat. She laid her hand over Elli's hand on the table. "I understand."

"Do you, really?"

"Yes," Mallory assured her. "I see how it all happened and why."

"How kind of you, Danner. Third understands, too. He's always been loving, thoughtful and helpful to me." She smiled. "I've been just as tolerant of his romantic shenanigans. I hope you won't judge him too harshly before you get to know him better."

Mallory felt compelled to admit, "I do have a negative opinion from everything I've read about him."

"It's all true," said Elli without hesitation. "But believe me, half his 'conquests' lead the way to his bed. The other half beg to be led. To his credit, none of them ever says a disparaging word about him in private or in print."

Mallory couldn't recall any bad press from his lady friends, but wondered again about Michelle, the maid. If questioned about West, what would Michelle say?

Elli chuckled as if amused by Mallory's dubious silence. "Oh, yes, he's a scamp, but a gentleman at heart. He never left my side when I had a minor stroke last year. Reserve judgment a while longer if you can."

"I'll do my best, Mrs. C."

"So much for memory lane," Elli said, gathering up the new Hermès handbag and kidskin gloves she'd bought earlier at Saks. "Let's go to Gump's. I haven't been there in forty years."

WEST CAME bicycling into the driveway just as Mallory drove his car through the gate. Elli rolled down her window and waved at him.

"Pedal to the metal, Angel," he challenged through the window. "Race me to the garage."

She shook her head, but Elli overruled her. "Do it, Danner."

Mallory felt a thrill speed up her spine. "Is that an order, Mrs. C.?"

"Yes. Pull out the stops," Elli commanded, tightening her seat belt. "On your mark, Third. Get set, you two. Aaaand go!"

Mallory didn't cut West any slack. She geared up from first to second to third, plunging his sports car forward in a burst of speed. He stood on his pedals, pumped furiously, switched through his gears—and lost ground to his own car.

Elli turned her head to view him through the rear window. "Screech the tires at the finish line, Danner. Smoke him!"

Mallory did more than smoke him. She jerked the steering wheel sharply to her left and made the rear fishtail to the right. Then jerked right for a swerve to the left.

Then something devilish—daredevilish—rose in her. Or maybe it was only her special training in the art of evasive driving. Whatever the stimulus, the response was irresistible.

Yelling "Hang on!" she spun the car into a tight half circle, then straightened it out again. With more space, she could have gone hog wild in a full doughnut.

Elli shrieked, "Wheee!"

Inches from the garage door, Mallory braked to a squealing, screeching, smoking stop.

"Show-off," West breathlessly accused moments later. Gasping for air and laughing at the same time, he took off his helmet and dismounted. "Still in one piece, Aunt?"

"Having the time of my life," Elli declared. "Danner, you're a wonder."

"And a speed demon, too," West said, seeing an exhilarated, saucy sparkle in Mallory's eyes. He opened the passenger door and assisted his aunt out of the car.

"Help Danner with my packages," she told him. "I've got to find the ladies' room. Too much tea." She hurried into the house.

West fixed Mallory with a commanding gaze. "Stay where you are, Angel. I'll get your door for you. To the victor, the spoils."

Hoping her skirt would ride up when he handed her out of his low-slung car, he came to her door and opened it.

"Butlers are supposed to help themselves out of automobiles," she advised, placing her hand in the hand he offered to her.

With one eye on her hemline, he drew her out of the driver's seat. Ah, what smooth, delicate knees! Then he noticed that her eyes were straying to his bike shorts. He had dressed to ride, not to catch her attention, but he certainly didn't mind getting an admiring look. Her body, her sexuality and everything else about her interested him just as much. More every day.

"Who taught you to drive like a demon, Angel?"

"My father. Evasive driving techniques were part of my butler/bodyguard training."

"Karate on wheels."

"In a way," she agreed, biting into her lower lip. "May I have my hand back?"

"Not yet. Flip me karate-style. Show me how you do it."

Once again, he was tempting her, spurring her on. Again, she couldn't resist. She slipped the car keys from her other hand into her pocket.

"You're asking for it, West."

"Give it to me, Angel."

She took a stance, balanced her weight and neatly flipped him flat on his back.

He lay on the asphalt, grinning up at her and holding a hand out. "Help me get up."

She curled her fingers around his and tugged upward. As he pulled downward, she lost her balance and toppled over on him.

"West!" Mallory sprawled on his long, hard body, staring helplessly into his laughing eyes. "You did that on purpose!"

"You fell," he argued, holding her tight. "All I've done is catch you. If you want me to let go, I will." He relaxed his hold convincingly. "But if you don't . . ."

Mallory didn't, and she couldn't deny it. It was wildly improper to wallow in West's impromptu embrace, but getting up and out of it was getting hard to do. She wanted to whisper *Hold me tighter. Kiss me. Make me do wilder, crazier things than I've ever let myself do.*

"What do we do now?" West murmured, shifting suggestively under her. "Kiss, for starters?"

"Yes—" She gulped and quickly retracted, "I mean, no. I—"

"A little one wouldn't even smear your lipstick," he coaxed, smooching his lips together playfully.

Mallory almost let herself get smooched. His mouth had all the power of a megamagnet. But just before the point of no return, she lifted her head and pulled a breath of air into her lungs.

"I think I'd better get up," she gasped.

He frowned. "Already?"

"Before it's too late." She summoned back the resistance she'd lost, rolled off of him and got back on her feet.

"It's never too late." He came to his feet and promptly took her hand again. "You don't mind if I just hold it, do you?"

West was gratified to feel her fingers tremble and to see her look uncertain. Circling one finger over her palm, he murmured, "You interest me to no end, you know."

She knew. In no time at all, West had brought out the mischief in her. It was a relief, but regret was also setting in. Not to mention the guilty feeling she always got whenever she forgot her responsibilities and had too much of a good time.

"Your interest in women is legendary, you know," she parried, groping to recover her professional composure and sense of duty. "The ceiling mirror in your bedroom has kept the maids whispering and giggling since the first day."

West grinned. "And how did you react? I'd like to hear that you visualized your own reflection in it."

She had visualized it, all right—in lusty, wanton detail. But she kept a straight face so he wouldn't get a hint of what she had pictured herself doing with him. In his king-size bed. Under his overhead mirror.

She tried to slide her fingers away from his, but he held on gently. "West . . ."

"I have something for you, Angel." He reached into his shirt pocket and brought out a key ring with a silver heart attached. He placed it in her palm and folded her fingers over it. "A little memento of Valentine's Day."

"Why, thank you." Mallory felt flustered and pleased. "But you shouldn't have."

"I don't want you to forget our first date, Angel."

"It wasn't a date, West." She slid her hand out of his slowly, reluctant to part from his warm touch, and gave him his car keys. "We'd better take Mrs. C.'s purchases inside. The trunk and front cubby are full."

"Putting me at a distance again, Angel?" He stepped away to unlock the car trunk. "Wounding my male ego without a trace of pity?"

"You tease me without a trace of mercy," she bantered, drawing a hatbox out from behind the front seat. *You make me tease you back, too. More and more, you big rascal.*

"You know what teasing really is, Angel?"

"No. What?"

He winked and replied, "Foreplay."

5

A VITAL PART of Mallory's job was quality control, so she made regular checks of the work the household staff performed. Under her direction, Berthe followed sound rules of housekeeping and directly supervised Rosa, Edith and Pearl. But since the buck in a sizable staff of servants always stopped at the butler, Mallory kept them on their toes.

She began each day early in the kitchen, conferring with the cook and his assistant. Ardent movie fans, the two went by nicknames they'd chosen from James Bond films: Q and Oddjob. Quirky, but easier than having anyone pronounce their tongue-twisting Hungarian names.

Mallory then carried a cup of hot chocolate and a freshly ironed newspaper up to Ellinor's second-floor suite. Elli was always awake, sitting up in bed, with the TV in her bedroom tuned to the all-news channel.

This morning, Elli was laughing at a cat-food commercial when Mallory entered with the paper and chocolate.

"Good morning, Mrs. C. What's so funny?"

"I've decided to have cats. Three or four of them, all past the kitten stage but not full grown. Where can I get them?"

"The city animal shelter always has orphans."

Elli snapped her fingers, indicating it was just the thing. "Please go there for me and adopt four orphans for good measure. I'm afraid if I go along, I'll want to bring home every one, which isn't practical now, is it? So you go and choose. I trust your judgment."

"I'll do it right away." Mallory made a mental note to put cat supplies on the kitchen grocery list.

Elli patted the edge of the bed. "Sit down for a moment. I have something more to ask of you. A special, personal request."

Mallory sat on the indicated spot. It wasn't a proper butler's place, but Elli wasn't a great stickler for tradition.

"Now," said Elli, "when we started out more than a week ago, our understanding was that Third wouldn't be here often. Yet he's been here every day since."

"I noticed that," Mallory said.

"And he hasn't been out at night on dates or had any vistors," Elli added.

Mallory didn't mention that West had spent some part of each day flirting with the butler. One day she had found a perfect red rosebud from him in her message box. Today there'd been a little candy bouquet of chocolate kisses. As well, he had seemed to make a point of strolling around in his bike shorts before and after his daily ride.

However, it was true that he'd spent every night but last night dining, reading, playing cards and watching TV with Elli. Surprising, to say the least.

"It's not like him, Danner, except for him going out last evening. And that was only to his men's club's new-member initiation. He goes once every year and ties one on."

Mallory had wondered where he'd gone. She'd also wondered whether he had returned alone.

"They have a big cake at the initiation bash," Elli went on, "with a different exotic dancer bursting out of the top layer each year. West always brings her back with him. Every year."

"Hmm." Mallory was too disconcerted to muster any articulate response. She felt a pang of disappointment—almost outright jealousy—that West had flirted relentlessly with her all week, yet had brought a bimbo to his bed last night. She tried hard to amuse herself with the idea that the maids would find cake frosting in his bedsheets today.

"'Hmm' is the word, Danner, because I'm certain he came home alone last night." Elli smiled brilliantly. "I think he's turning over a new leaf, don't you?"

"I'm not that familiar with his habits, Mrs. C." Mallory held back her own brilliant smile and kept a straight face. *He didn't bring anyone home!*

Not that she should be feeling sky-high about it or thinking it had anything to do with her. She had to remember that he was a world-class flirt, a Beatty-before-Bening bad boy. What earthly good would it do her to join the ranks of his conquests? She could imagine him conquering her, though, without any trouble at all.

"Do what you can for his hangover later this morning," Elli instructed. "Take him a pot of strong coffee and plenty of aspirin around noon, and make sure the maids don't disturb him. A man needs a butler the morning after a bash."

"Coffee and aspirin," Mallory agreed, rising from the bed. "Anything else?"

Elli sipped her hot chocolate and waved a hand. "Nothing more."

MALLORY WENT to the downtown animal shelter and adopted four half-grown cats in Ellinor Cade's name. The two females and two males had to be vaccinated and neutered first, so she would return the next day to bring them home.

"Some cats get the lucky breaks," the shapely adoption clerk sighed as Mallory was leaving. "Some butlers, too. Is West Cade as cute as his pictures?"

Mallory wasn't so sure that working where West Cade lived was a lucky break. The clerk would never believe that he was Mallory's biggest, baddest problem. Being a perfect butler around him was a contest of wills.

Yesterday he had clipped a fashion article about short skirts out of the newspaper and slipped it into her pocket when she'd passed him in the hall. Another day he had put a little gift envelope in her message box. It had contained a barrette exactly like the one she always wore on the job, except that the gift barrette had the clip-spring removed. It was useless for holding her hair back—his point, precisely.

He was always on her mind; she was always on her slippery guard. And now she had to visit his bedroom—with him in it.

Carrying coffee and aspirin upstairs on a silver tray, Mallory reviewed what to do if she found a woman in bed with West. He might have gotten one in without Mrs. C. knowing.

Don't acknowledge his bedmate's presence unless she speaks to you. Pour coffee for them both as if nothing could be more natural. Open the curtains, make a polite comment about the weather, and leave quietly. If he or she is nude, don't stare. Don't even sneak a peek.

Above all, Mallory Danner, do not feel betrayed.

She knocked on the door of West's suite and waited a moment. There was no sugar frosting smeared on the door. So far, so good. Entering his living room, she spoke softly.

"Mr. Cade?"

Hearing no orgasmic screams or shouts, she progressed to his bedroom door and knocked again, then opened it an inch.

"Mr. Cade?" she whispered. No sounds of bedsprings to be heard. No soft, shivery sighs, either. Still, there was no telling what she'd find inside.

Braced for the worst, she pushed open the door and entered West's dark, private domain. He was alone in his king-size bed, facedown and apparently nude. No bimbo bubbled in the bathtub. No show of polite ignorance toward her would be necessary.

Only West's bare backside required polite ignorance. Tray in hand, spine ruler straight, Mallory crossed the room and yanked the curtains open, sneaking several peeks at his buns.

"Good morning, sir."

Allowing West several moments to wake and cover himself, she looked out the window and recalled the last time she'd had a hangover. The two-year-old memory was still painful. She heard West move in the bed, moan, then utter a pithy opinion of the sunshine streaming into his room.

"Well said," she told him approvingly. Judging it safe to turn around, she pivoted on one heel and made a breathtaking discovery.

West didn't have any tan lines on the entire front of his nude body! He was up on one elbow, rubbing his eyes, the original Adam in the sunshine of paradise.

Mallory stared. She'd never seen any man like him—lithe, lean and suntanned all over, with crisp, curly hair on his chest and more of it down around his eye-popping—

She caught herself and looked up, straight at his face. He was gazing at her with bleary, bloodshot eyes. He winked and grinned. To her relief, he drew the sheet over his hips and propped himself up against his pillows.

"'S that you, Angel?"

"Yes," she whispered. She took a deep breath, steadied her balance and went to set the tray on his bedside table. "Mrs. C. sent me with reinforcements."

"You're an angel of mercy," he murmured. "Thanks for whispering."

"Shall I bring breakfast in a while?"

"I don't know. Let me think . . . if I can."

"Take your time."

He blinked at her in the sunshine, then groaned and patted the edge of his bed. "Sit down."

"West, I don't think—"

"Sit. Please." He grimaced and put his hands to his head, as if holding it steady. "You look like triplets on a merry-go-round."

She sat on the edge and poured him a cup of coffee. "Here. Try this to clear your head."

He took the cup and drained it in two gulps, then settled back and looked at her. "Pour me another. You're twins now, on a roller coaster."

"Have two aspirin," she said after refilling his cup and serving it to him.

"I'd rather have you, Angel." He swallowed the tablets she gave him. "Just you."

Mallory made herself look out the window instead of straight at the thick hair on his bare chest or at his pebble-point nipples encircled by the hair. The time was perfect to make a polite comment about the weather.

"A beautiful day for a bike ride."

He groaned in reply and had another swig of coffee. "Why can't I get to first base with you?" He set the cup on the tray and settled back to frown at her. "Where do I go wrong, no matter what I do?"

Mallory opened her mouth to calmly enumerate every reason a prude and a playboy could never, ever mix. To her astonishment, she blurted, "You don't go wrong. You make me wish . . ."

She clapped her fingers over her mouth and mumbled through them, "I mean, we can never, ever . . ."

She saw his eyes widen and glint. He was leaning toward her, clasping her wrist, drawing her hand away from her face.

"Whatever you wish," he was murmuring, "I'll make it come true."

He draped her hand over his shoulder and she felt his powerful muscles flex. His skin felt warm and smooth. *No tan lines.* She could feel his arm snake around her waist and pull her close. His breath held the rich scent of coffee. He was going to kiss her and she knew she wasn't poised to stop him.

Equilibrium was deserting her, speeding away. Desire was flooding up and a devil somewhere within was making her yearn for a wild taste of paradise.

She closed her eyes as his lips touched hers, melted hers, made her wish it would never end. There had never been this much bliss in a kiss, never this rampant, ravenous delight. His tongue slid into her mouth, where it played all around before it lured her tongue to play in his.

He made a sound, a yearning moan, which Mallory felt vibrate into her. She became aware of his fingers undoing the bow tie of her blouse.

"Angel-Angel-Angel," he was murmuring against her lips.

"No-no-no," she gasped. Her head was spinning and she could feel her knees knocking.

West pulled, and her bow came untied. He dipped his lips lower and kissed the hollow of her throat. He polished her pounding pulse with his tongue.

"Yes, Angel."

"I . . . West . . . noooo . . ."

Mallory forced herself out of his embrace and pushed herself off the bed. She bumped against the bedside table on her way to her feet. The silver pot and tray clattered against each other. Coffee slopped out of the cup.

Fumbling to tie up her bow, she wobbled a few steps away and turned her back to the bed. She couldn't think of a thing to say.

"Take it easy," West said. "What's so bad about having a good time?"

"Everything," she replied, shaken and showing it. "I'm a butler." *Not a bimbo.* "This is not what I'm being paid to do."

Damn the blouse! It wouldn't tie into a bow. Her knees wouldn't quit noodling, either. Where had her professional grip gone? *Always friendly, never familiar.* Didn't she wish . . .

"Angel, come here and sit down. I'll tie that for you."

"No."

"Look, I pulled it loose. Let me do it up again."

She mangled it into a lopsided knot and turned to face him. That was another mistake, because West had a powerful erection his sheet couldn't hide. Infuriatingly, he made no move to raise one knee or turn on his side. He just opened his hands in appeal, looking sexy and helpless.

"Sex springs eternal," he said.

Mallory took up the tray and staggered past him, trying to keep the pot and cup and aspirin container on an even keel. At the door she paused, but didn't look back.

"Let's both forget this, West, and just go on as if nothing happened. All right?"

"I never kiss and tell," he said, "but I'll *never* forget how you kiss. Will that do?"

"Well enough." She'd never forget how he kissed, either, but telling him right out would be one more mistake.

It didn't help any to hear him chuckle as she hurried out of his suite with her professional dignity in ruins.

As soon as Mallory left, West stopped chuckling and started feeling more uneasy than he'd ever felt in his life. Being hung over contributed to the feeling, but that wasn't the root cause.

It was Mallory. After all this time, she was still eluding him. He couldn't remember having to woo a woman that long before winning her. Three days was the maximum, no matter who the woman was. Two days was average.

Damn it all! Was he losing his golden touch? He looked up at himself in the mirror and found at least one thing encouraging in his reflection: his sex drive wasn't letting him down.

But so what? Mallory hadn't seemed to think much of it, hadn't shown any lusty interest in making the most of it. Maybe he'd been all wrong about the devil in Danner.

He heard a knock on his outer door. *Has the devil in her changed her mind?*

"Come right back in," he called.

"Third, it's Aunt. Are you among the living yet?"

"Oh. Yeah, more or less." He lifted his knees to tent the sheet.

Elli breezed into his bedroom. She went to the window and looked out, then turned and skewered him with an unblinking gaze. "I saw Danner zoom out of here a moment ago. May I ask why?"

"No," he said, "but thanks for sending her in with French roast and aspirin."

"You weren't naughty or anything?"

"Not on purpose, Aunt."

"Third, I hope you realize that Danner is a lady, apart from being a splendid butler. She has high morals and standards that shouldn't be taken lightly."

"Aunt, you're badgering my hangover."

Elli clucked her tongue. She came over and pinched his cheek. "I'm badgering *you*. I'd have Danner bring you some breakfast, but she'll be too busy helping me find a ball costume in the attic and giving me a dance lesson in the ballroom. I need to learn some modern dance steps."

"I wouldn't mind if she taught me the lambada," West mused.

Elli arched a brow. "Knowing you, it's a kissing cousin of this dirty dancing I've been hearing about."

"You know me best, Aunt."

"I know I'd like to see more of your better, nobler side, Third. Would you show more to Danner, for my sake if nothing else? I don't want her quitting the job because of you, or for any other reason."

"I'll try to find something nobler than usual in myself, Aunt."

She tweaked his cheek again and tousled his hair. "You'll be surprised by what you find if you dig deeply enough."

AFTER SERVING LUNCH and giving Ellinor a dancing lesson, Mallory went up to the attic with her and the three maids to unpack and sort through several cedar trunks of costumes.

Mallory was relieved that West hadn't appeared for lunch. He came up to the attic, though, claiming to be looking for his aunt.

At any rate, the maids perked up the moment he walked in wearing sea-green bike shorts, a *Tour de France* T-shirt, and open-fingered bike gloves.

"Hello, Mr. Third," they trilled, a trio of admirers. "How are you?"

He shaded his eyes with both hands. "Blinded by beauty, ladies. How are *you*?"

They twittered together, "Fine, thank you."

Mallory refrained from gagging at how little it took for West to make Edith, Rosa and Pearl giggle like schoolgirls.

"How's Aunt's invaluable butler?" he said.

"Fine, thank you." Mallory almost dropped the fairy-godmother gown she was holding up for Elli to look at.

"Third, what do you think of this airy-fairy dress for me? I wore it long ago at a *Midsummer Night's Dream* party. With rhinestone slippers and a magic wand, will I enchant one and all at my ball?"

"Without even trying," he confirmed. "What should I go as? Dracula? Batman?"

A wry imp in Mallory couldn't resist suggesting, "Casanova? Don Juan?"

Elli laughed loudly and the maids joined in.

West laughed, too, then winked at Mallory and gibed, "*You* could go as a Puritan."

"Did you come up here just to tease everyone, Third?" Elli asked.

"No, I've decided to get my trip under way, day after tomorrow. Thought you'd want to know in advance."

Mallory saw the maids and Elli look disappointed, half crushed to hear West's news. She hoped her own face didn't betray anything but polite neutrality.

She should be glad he was leaving. Glad he wouldn't be popping up everywhere after tomorrow. She could get him off her mind and do her job without him undoing her bow tie.

She shouldn't feel disappointed and half-crushed. Yet she did.

6

"THAT'S IT, Mrs. C.," Mallory said approvingly. "Step-slide-step-pause."

Teaching Elli the latest dance steps would have been easier without four playful, half-grown cats underfoot. Goldfinger, Dr. No, Moneypenny and Octokitty—named by Q and Oddjob—were a nuisance but Elli was a fool for the little troublemakers.

The females were calicoes, the males both tiger-striped grays. They had the run of the house, but always clustered around Elli as if aware that she was their personal savior and deserved their gratitude.

Mallory was fond of them, too, outside of the ballroom. On the dance floor, accidentally stepping on tails could result in bloodcurdling yowls, especially from Moneypenny.

Ellinor paused in midstep to watch the video dance program Mallory was using to teach her the Texas two-step. "Danner, please make a note for the orchestra to play this tune at the ball. The guests who come dressed in Old West costumes will like it." She fanned her face with her hand.

"Let's take a breather, Mrs. C."

"Yes, I need one."

Mallory smiled. Elli looked so cute in her electric-blue leotard and tights.

"I might even take up ballet after this," Elli said, going up on tiptoes in her new Reeboks. "I had classes as a child. Not too old yet, I hope."

Mallory shook her head. "Not if you're young at heart. Shall I bring some lemonade from the kitchen for you?"

"None for me. Would you like some?"

"No, I'm just fine. I—" Mallory broke off, her eye caught by someone strolling into the spacious ballroom. A *pirate*—replete with buccaneer boots, bandana, black eye patch, one gold earring and a parrotlike bird perched on his shoulder. Swarthy and swashbuckling, brandishing a dagger, West swaggered across the polished parquet floor.

"Yo-ho-ho and a barrel of rum," he growled, leering melodramatically at Moneypenny.

She responded by rubbing her whiskers on his boots. Dr. No raised up on hind legs to have a good look at the bird. It puffed up its brilliant scarlet, green, blue and yellow feathers and verbalized a loud warning at the cats.

"Beat it!"

"Third, where did you get these pirate things?"

"A costume shop. I wore everything home just for fun."

Elli circled her forefinger in the air. "Turn around— show us all sides. What kind of parrot?"

"Not a parrot, a green-wing macaw." He made two turns for Elli, then unleashed a wicked grin at Mallory.

"Would ye like to see me skull and crossbones, pretty lass?"

"I feel seasick already, Captain," Mallory replied.

"Foxy lady," the macaw pronounced, scrutinizing her with one of its round, fishlike eyes.

West laughed. "Meet Beakins. He belongs to the singles bar next to the costume shop. I rented him for the afternoon and reserved him for the ball. The bar customers have taught him every word he knows."

Mallory was unable to smother a delighted smile or stop her heart from flipping over and over on itself. West was breathtaking, a fantasy prince of pirates. He seemed to have carried the salt tang and high adventure of the seven seas right into the ballroom with him.

She began feeling dull and dowdy in her gray warm-up suit. Not a "pretty lass" or a "foxy lady" at all. No match for the bold, dashing rogue whose sea-green eye held a lusty gleam.

"I'm thirsty," Elli said, fanning her face again and moving away at a fast pace. "I'll go find a lemonade in the kitchen."

She scurried off, followed by the cats, before Mallory could say a discouraging word.

"Will ye miss me when I'm gone to sea, me pretty?" West inquired.

Beakins let forth an ear-splitting wolf whistle.

"I'd miss anyone in the household who left for a while," Mallory replied, "you included."

"But will ye *miss* me, lass?"

"Always teasing, aren't you, West?" She turned away to switch off the video.

"Not always, Angel." He took her arm and made her face him again. "I stop when I apologize, and I'm sorry I teased you into breaking your rules of order the other morning. Maybe I was still sort of drunk or something."

"I'm sure I was at fault, too," she admitted. "Nothing more needs to be said about it."

"Aunt would kill me if you resigned because I harassed you. Do you think I did?"

"No. I just think you're more full of...well, fun than any man I've ever dealt with. I realize that having any woman you want has never posed any problem for you."

"I want *you*, Angel. Hiding it isn't easy."

"West, I'm not easy. I don't romp around in bed with my employers' nephews."

He looked mildly offended. "Didn't you like our kiss?"

Beakins exclaimed, "Kiss my assets!"

"You know I did," she said, unable to stifle a smile, "and you know why it can't happen again. There are rules that can't be broken where a butler is concerned."

She paused, feeling ludicrous about lecturing a lawless pirate and his mouthy macaw on the rules of proper behavior.

"I'm listening," West prompted. He sheathed his dagger, as if to convince her.

"Servants have radar ears," she said, "and sooner or later they pick up everything that goes on in a household."

It was an effort to recall that she wasn't speaking to the captain of a pirate galleon. His wide-sleeved shirt, open to his waist, made his broad chest a tempting sight.

Struggling to stay on track, she continued, "Any personal involvement with you will undermine my authority. If everyone I manage here found out, no one would obey my orders. They'd slack off at work. They—"

"Would you at least teach me to dance?"

"What?" She blinked, disoriented by his unexpected question.

"Dance. I'll be all feet at the ball otherwise."

He turned away, perched Beakins on the branch of a potted palm and started looking through the assortment of dance videos Mallory had rented for Elli.

"I . . . if you're leaving tomorrow, teaching you to dance doesn't make sense. It takes more than one lesson. Mrs. C. will return any moment now, anyway."

"Until she comes back," he said, holding up one of the cassettes. "How about this? Pirate Jigs for Beginners."

Mallory cracked another smile, for the title was actually Dirty Dancing for Beginners. Ellinor had specially requested that video from the rental list. Her lengthening absence—and this one sexy dance tape—raised Mallory's sudden suspicion that she'd been set up.

But then Elli popped through the ballroom doorway with a portable phone in her hand. "I have a call, from an old friend."

"Is it okay if Angel gives me a lesson, Aunt?"

"Perfectly all right. Give him a whirl, Danner. I won't be back for a long while." Chatting into the phone, she popped out of the doorway.

"There," West said smugly. "Now you've got orders and permission both."

"I'm not going to dirty-dance with you, West. Waltz, yes. Fox-trot, fine. But not—"

"You're no fun, Angel. Whose authority will fall apart if we do a hot number together? It's everyone's day off but yours, so the radar is shut down."

Mallory could feel him instantly undermining her resolve. True, the household staff was having a day off. True, there was no one to see or know, especially if Elli wouldn't be back for "a long while."

"I never kiss and tell, remember?" he softly persisted. "Or ever dance and tell, either."

Swayed by West's expert salesmanship, Mallory wavered and weakened. He was soft-selling her a chance to dirty dance with a bold seafarer, and the devil in her was getting sold on the idea.

"One lesson, then" she heard the tiny demon say before she could muzzle it.

West loaded the tape into the VCR and took her into his arms. "Come, lass. Set sail with me."

"Aye-aye, Captain."

Mallory was aware of fitting perfectly in his embrace. She felt his arm close around her until he was holding her tight against his tall body. His strength was hard and commanding. His warm hand held hers in a classic waltz position for a moment, then drew inward and flattened her hand on his chest.

She was enthralled to feel crisp hair tickling her palm and fingers. Then he moved his hips to the heavy beat of the introductory music, seducing her to move hers. Her pulse took up the beat and began drumming in her ears. She was body to body with a rash, reckless rover and it was a heady thrill to set sail with him over the smooth sea of the parquet floor.

It didn't seem to matter that he apparently had two left feet. His hips made up for that, undulating sinuously to the beat, matching her own hips move for move.

"Lass," she heard him murmur in her ear, "you're shivering me timbers and killing me self-control."

She dimly thought that he was unfairly accusing her. He was guilty of rocking her foundations and her world order. He was making her forget who she was and where. With him, in his arms, she was a woman she had never been before. Yes, a saucy, flirtatious lass with no reservations about being this rapscallion's willing captive. Yes, a bewitching creature as exciting as the pirate himself.

Yes!

Lacing her fingers behind his neck, she let her head fall back, closed her eyes and reveled in the fantasy. He was unclipping her barrette and she made a breathy sound of delight and encouragement. His fingers wove through her hair, fluffing it, setting it free. Then his hands cradled her head and she opened her eyes.

She saw his black eye patch, his lusty green eye. His parted lips captured hers and she almost swooned as his tongue thrust in and plundered her mouth. She kissed him back with equal fervor and fierce abandon, hoping to intoxicate his senses as he was intoxicating hers.

Somewhere faraway, there was the video dance instructor, explaining basic steps and variations. Mallory shut that world out and gave herself up to her dance partner. He was bending her backward over one of his strong arms, nuzzling her neck, darting the tip of his tongue against her skin. One of his lean, long thighs was wedged between her thighs and he was making her ache for him to touch and kiss her breasts.

She offered them up to him and his free hand took every advantage. Stroking and kneading, his finger-tips aroused the sensitive tips until she was breathlessly caressing his chest the same way.

"More," he groaned, sliding the zipper of her top down. "I need more of you. I can't stop."

"Don't stop," she gasped as his fingers dipped into her bra and cupped one breast. His thumb circled the crest slowly, made it taut and tight.

He pushed the stretch cup down and kissed her there, then closed his lips over her and sucked gently. "You're so beautiful" she heard him murmur against her tender, swollen nipple. "I have to have you. Have to, Angel."

Angel. Hearing West's pet name for her, Mallory slowly opened her eyes and more slowly remembered who she was—and who he was. She wasn't a saucy lass without a care in the world. Not a pirate's wanton. Not his willing captive.

She heard Beakins suddenly demand, "Read my lips."

His raucous squawk brought full awareness rushing back. She was a professional butler and the man feasting on her bare, heaving bosom was her employer's nephew.

"West," she gasped, pushing him away weakly. "Stop . . . cover me up . . . put me back in my . . ."

"Back in your straitjacket?" he asked in a thick voice, raising his head to look into her eyes. "Angel, I know you want to be free. We both want—"

"We can't," she protested, but couldn't quite pull out of his arms. "We just...can't." Nonetheless, some part of her remained captivated enough that she stayed wrapped in his embrace without a struggle.

"We can," he countered. "There's nothing I want more than you right now. Just you."

West was well aware of having said those exact words to scores of beautiful women over the years. He'd always sort of meant it when he'd said it, but now he was aware of really meaning every single word.

He felt obsessed with the woman he held in his arms. She had become the sole focus of his attention day after day, so much so that playing the field hadn't appealed to him once since he'd met her.

He heard the music on the video segue into "Hungry Eyes." His ravenous gaze was riveted on Mallory. She had the most beautiful face, hair, eyes and body in the world. And kissing her lips, not to mention her pink-tipped breast, seemed to have wiped out his memory of kissing anyone else. She was delicious.

He heard her saying "West, please." She was easing her bra back into place. "Mrs. C. could walk in at any moment. We have to get a grip on ourselves."

West had the sudden sensation that he had lost something more than his grip in the past few moments. Trying to get it back might be a better idea than losing any more of it—whatever it was.

"Maybe we did go overboard," he conceded, zipping up her top and loosening his passionate hold on her. He couldn't make himself release her yet. Besides, she seemed to need the steadying support of his hands around her slender waist.

He couldn't quite unglue his attention from her face, either. She was a vision of beauty with her coppery curls falling wild and free to her shoulders. Her gray eyes were enormous and darker than usual. *Hungry Eyes.*

"Well," he managed to say. "Thanks for the dance."

She nodded and dropped her gaze. West saw it stop just below his belt buckle. He saw her lashes flutter and a colorful flush rise to her cheeks.

"Just a few hormones acting up," he quipped, feeling unnaturally apologetic and self-conscious about his all-too-apparent virility.

She shook her head, as if at herself. "All my fault," she murmured. "Again."

"Angel, it took two to dirty-dance. Don't get an ulcer over it. I sure won't." He released her reluctantly and perched Beakins on his shoulder. "Let's go, Beak."

"Go," the macaw parroted. "Go to hell."

West left the ballroom, laughing. The only way to go.

AFTER WEST TOOK OFF early the next day, Mallory plunged her energy into the million and one things that had to be done in preparation for the ball. He would be gone for two weeks and had promised Elli that he'd return in time for the event.

Although each day was hectic from dawn to bedtime, Mallory wasn't able to block West out of her mind. She went about her duties, picturing him on an exotic island, imagining herself sunning nude in paradise with him. Over and over in her mind, she relived her experience in the ballroom with him.

Her weekly phone call to Dad was an effort, although it had always been a chatty, pleasant interlude before. She forestalled any probing queries by telling Dad all about the ball preparations. He only got three and a half questions in edgewise.

"How must you store the oysters you'll serve, Lory?"

"Rounded side down, of course."

"Name a top quality cigar."

"Monte Cristo."

"What murders the flavor of Champagne?"

"Chocolate. Never serve them together."

"Has West Cade tried to sedu—?"

"Moneypenny! Bad kitty! She's clawing the tapestries again, Dad. Got to run stop her. 'Bye."

And so it went. There was much to be done: a dance orchestra and jazz combo to be hired, flowers and decorations to be decided upon, a parking valet needed to assist the chauffeur, temporary footmen to help serve cocktails.

Elli wanted a skit for entertainment, so Mallory hired four actors to improvise a comedy. It would be a silly farce in which Ellinor would play fairy godmother to a bumbling Prince Charming, an airhead Cinderella and two brainless court jesters.

Always, in the midst of it all, Mallory missed West and the opportunities he had provided for her to tap into her wild side. Before meeting West, she had so often wished to be as free-spirited and adventurous as she'd been in childhood. But being a parent figure at an early age—and becoming a butler later on—had dammed up her ability to let herself go.

Her experiences with West had been unexpected breakthroughs, exciting and sensual, thrilling moments of fun.

Elli summoned her one day and inquired whether West had telephoned.

"No, not so far."

"He hasn't written, either," Elli fretted. "It's not like him. He's always phoned me in the past, sometimes twice a day, to make sure I'm all right. But, then, he's probably thinking that I'm no longer depressed, and he knows I'm in capable hands. Yours, Danner."

"I'm sure there's no reason to worry, Mrs. C."

Elli raised one eyebrow. "You two didn't have any misunderstanding before he left, I hope."

"No." Mallory shook her head. "None at all."

"Well, that's comforting to know. He seemed subdued the last morning at breakfast. You were less lively, too. I couldn't help but wonder... and worry that his dance lesson hadn't gone well."

Too well, Mallory thought. "I think he found the lesson helpful."

"How did you find it, Danner?"

To Mallory's relief, the doorbell rang. "It must be the florist, even though I told him three times to ring at the service entrance."

"Yes, he never listens." Elli waved a hand, excusing her. "Put Third straight through to me if he calls."

THE EVENING of the ball arrived and West still hadn't phoned or returned home.

Dressed in a black tuxedo, Mallory made a thorough inspection of the house and the hired help, then did a last-minute check of the kitchen.

It was a whirlwind of activity, where Q and Oddjob were putting the finishing touches on a splendid, eclectic buffet: Tomales Bay oysters and Russian caviar, nasturtium *salade*, Portola Valley quail eggs, lobster and *foie gras*, Mediterranean lamb, duckling Santa Fe.

And that was only the half of it. For dessert they'd made meringues, tortes and crepes suzette. The Veuve Clicquot was chilled to the perfect degree for champagne, other fine wines had been uncellared, hard spirits and brandies were ready to be served.

Mallory could hear the cocktail jazz combo and the ballroom orchestra tuning up. Crystal chandeliers were lit and glittering. In minutes the ball would begin.

Coming into the main entry, she met Pearl hurrying down the stairs. "Miss Danner, Mrs. Cade needs you right now!"

"Is something wrong, Pearl?"

"Nothing bad. Missus is all dressed and ready, but she needs her jitters calmed down. I can't tame butterflies like you can."

"I'll go right up, Pearl. Exciting night, isn't it?"

Pearl's eyes sparkled as she continued down the stairs. "Just like the best fairy tale, Miss Danner."

The only thing missing, Mallory thought going up, *is the prince.*

"Well, if it isn't Mr. Third!" she heard Pearl exclaim behind her an instant later. "Look at you!"

Mallory's heart struck an erratic, upbeat tempo as West's voice replied, "Yo-ho-ho Pearl of my heart. Did you miss me one little bit?"

Pearl could be heard giggling as she answered, "Every day, Mr. Third. You look like a real, live pirate."

Beakins could be heard sounding off, "Foxy lady."

"How's Aunt doing?"

"You'll have to ask her instead of me. She was in a tizzy all week, wishing you had called."

Mallory turned at the middle landing and glanced downstairs. She saw West looking up from the newel post, and he was eyeing her as if he were seeing a maiden to be ravished. She felt like Scarlett O'Hara being ogled by Rhett Butler on the stairs at Twelve Oaks.

"And what have we here?" West inquired, raising his black eye patch and aiming both his gleaming green eyes at her. "A Puritan?"

Pearl giggled again and scuttled away toward the kitchen. West chuckled deep in his throat. Beakins yawned.

"Did the Puritan miss me too?"

Answering him honestly was out of the question, Mallory decided. Showing the sudden joy she was feeling wouldn't be prudent, either.

"Mrs. C. may never forgive you for keeping her in suspense, West," she said, sidestepping the question.

He clucked his tongue and headed up the stairs toward her. "Scolding me already, Angel? Rapping my naughty knuckles before you've even said hello?"

"I'm only preparing you for the scolding Mrs. C. will give you."

"She won't thrash me when she hears I was out of phone range most of the time. She'll be glad I didn't call from the airport when I got here. Aunt loves surprises. Where are you going?"

"To Mrs. C. She sent for me."

"Taking the long way around, aren't you?" he inquired.

"The shortcut is blocked to keep guests from wandering up to your suite and Mrs. C.'s."

"You think of everything, Angel."

"That's my job, West."

He was following so closely behind her that she could feel his body heat through her tuxedo. She scented his cologne—bay rum. Perfect for a pirate, and perfectly enticing. Exciting. Entrancing.

"So, tell me the truth, lass. Did you miss me or not?"

"I hope you had a pleasant trip, Captain."

"I missed you, Angel."

"I missed you, too, Captain."

West decided to quit asking questions and savor his little victory. He hadn't intended to probe her emotions or admit to his own out loud. He had intended to play the suave, reckless rake all night. He had counseled himself not to show how hard it had been to stay away for two weeks without phoning at least once to hear Mallory's voice.

It had been more than hard, but he had done it. And he had played the field, too—up to a point.

Who'd ever believe that he'd wined and dined a half-dozen beautiful women while he'd been gone, yet hadn't bedded any of them? His reputation would be shot if word got around, if he didn't start acting like himself again.

But, then, maybe his six dates weren't anxious to broadcast that the Playboy of the Western World had done no more than bid them good-night at the door. He hadn't even kissed them, except for the one he'd kissed on the back of her hand.

Reaching Ellinor's door, Mallory said, "Why don't you go in first and make her day. I'll wait a few minutes out here and then knock."

"Make-my-day-make-my-day," Beakins chanted.

"Afraid that Aunt will tongue-lash me right in front of you?" West mocked.

"Hoping she *won't* tongue-lash you if I'm there to witness it?"

"Maybe," he replied, lowering his black patch over his eye. "Or maybe I don't want you out of my sight after not seeing you for two weeks."

There. He had managed to wink, grin and sound sincerely insincere. More like himself. If he could maintain the same tone and expression from now on, no one would suspect him of being infatuated with Mallory. Before long, he'd get over it. It had to be a passing thing, like hayfever or the flu.

"I'm sure you weren't pining away alone all that time," she murmured, knocking on Ellinor's door.

"If it's Danner, come in," Elli called.

"It's me, Mrs. C." Mallory opened the door and entered the parlor.

Elli spoke from the bedroom. "I can't go down there without Third at my side. You go down and receive for me, Danner. Inform the guests that I'm indisposed or something plausible."

"That shouldn't be necessary," Mallory said. She entered the bedroom and found Ellinor drooping dispiritedly in front of a cheval mirror. "Look who followed me up the stairs."

Elli whirled around, the diaphanous, iridescent skirts of her fairy-godmother costume floating around her. "Is it—?"

West strode in, the swashbuckling hero. "Who else, Aunt?"

"Third! You rascal you!"

Laughing, West perched Beakins atop the mirror, then lifted his tiny aunt up at the waist and swung her around in a dizzying circle. He set her down gently and kissed her on both cheeks.

"Aunt, you look dazzling. The belle of the ball."

"No, no," she protested, gleefully tweaking his gold earring. "Danner far outshines me. Isn't she stunning in her tuxedo?"

"Stunning," he agreed, giving Mallory a rakish once-over. "I panted all the way up the stairs behind her. She warned me that you're ready to cross me out of your will."

"I would," Elli said, "if you didn't have a fortune of your own. How else can I punish you for not calling or writing or—"

"I was leagues away from post offices and pay phones, gorgeous."

"You worried me, dear boy."

"I knew you were in good hands," he said, squeezing her shoulders and looking at Mallory.

Elli nodded. "I was." She took up her magic wand and clicked the heels of her rhinestone slippers together. "Let's go down and greet the guests."

West held one arm out for Elli to take and offered his other arm to escort Mallory. Mallory made herself decline. She stepped forward, as a butler should.

"I'll lead the way."

"I'll have to catch you later, then," she heard West murmur behind her.

Preceding them through the long upper hall and down the long, curving stairway, Mallory kept her spine ramrod straight. She had combed her hair back and pinned it into a sedate twist. Tiny onyx earrings and shirt studs were her only jewelry. She was determined to represent Ellinor with perfect comportment and impeccable demeanor tonight.

The butler sets the tone. The butler is proper, inscrutable, never at a loss.

The cardinal rules weren't easy to keep in mind with West following behind her. It felt so good to have him home again. She could hardly wait until he started teasing and bothering her in earnest.

He put spice into life and she felt spicy again. She touched one hand to her black silk bow tie, just to make sure the bow wasn't twisting askew or coming undone due to her brimming excitement.

West was back and he had missed her! She wanted to throw herself in his arms and give him dance lessons all night.

Of course, she knew she couldn't. He was still a happy-go-lucky playboy, and later on she'd have to beat it into her brain until it stuck.

But not right now. She was too happy.

The doorbell rang. Mallory smoothed her French cuffs and marched down the stairs to sweep the door open for the first guest of the evening.

Elli waved her magic wand. "Let the ball begin!"

"Great balls of fire!" Beakins exclaimed.

Mallory heard West laugh behind her. She laughed, too, the happiest-go-luckiest laugh in the world.

7

PEARL WAS RIGHT, Mallory thought midway through the gala evening. *Just like the best fairy tale.*

The cream of San Francisco society was gathered in the ballroom, having a splendid time and dancing to a Strauss waltz. The costumes were grand, among them Cleopatra and the King of Siam.

Only a few of the guests knew their hostess personally, but that hadn't kept anyone from attending. No, Ellinor was too seriously rich, her name too prominent, for even the snootiest guests to ignore the social and financial benefits of making an appearance.

Mallory observed them currying Elli's favor. She could see them hoping to divert some portion of her vast wealth into their pet causes and charities. Ellinor Cade's name on their guest lists would bring luster to their social status.

Yes, they would all scratch Ellinor Cade's back in the hope that she might, just might, scratch theirs.

Seeing Elli raise a gloved hand and motion to her, Mallory made a circuit of the ballroom to where Elli was.

"Would you say it's showtime, Danner?"

Mallory nodded. "I'll check backstage first."

"I'll join you in a few minutes," said Elli.

Mallory made her way to the stage, where the skit would be played out. She'd overseen the rehearsals during the week and a dress rehearsal today and knew the lines by heart. Arriving backstage, she found only the brainless jesters present. The two young comedians were twins, named Tim and Tom, dressed in identical jester costumes. She couldn't tell them apart.

"Bumblebum prince and airhead Cindy aren't here, yet," they told her.

"Not here?" She frowned and checked her pocket watch. "I thought you were all coming together."

The twins looked mystified. One said, "They changed their minds after rehearsal. Haven't seen them since."

"Everything else is ready to go," said the other. He gestured at the stage props, which were all in position.

There was a peacock chair "throne" for Elli, and a huge papier-mâché pumpkin on wheels. A host of glittery stars, puffy white clouds and varicolored rainbows hung from a blue silk canopy sky.

"We'd better phone them, then," Mallory said.

"We already did," said the twins. "No answer."

Mallory tried to think. "This is a fine fix."

"What fine fix?" she heard Ellinor inquire. She turned and found Elli peeking around the curtain. "I hate to tell you, Mrs. C., but Cinderella and the prince haven't shown up yet."

"Oh, dear." Ellinor slipped inside the curtain and joined them. "Where are they?"

"Maybe stuck in traffic somewhere," one twin suggested.

Elli blinked. "What shall we do? Wait! I've got it. Danner, you know everyone's lines. You be Cinderella. You're the same size as her costume. It's here, isn't it?"

"In the dressing room," Tim or Tom confirmed.

"I'll get Third to fill in. Hurry and change."

"West doesn't know the lines," Mallory protested, seeing a bigger farce than the skit looming ahead.

"That won't matter," Elli declared. "Our prince is a dum-dum, anyway."

One of the twins agreed, "Yeah, a bozo who'd need an offstage prompt every time he has a line." He brightened, counting quickly on his fingers. "The prince only has seven short lines. Tim and I could make cue cards."

Tim nodded. "Hey, let's make it part of the act to hold cue cards up in plain view. It might get a big laugh."

Mallory had a screaming desire to shout that the show would *not* go on. Not on these terms.

"The show *must* go on," said Elli. "What can the twins use for cue cards, Danner?"

Mallory tried not to think. She tried to keep her mind completely blank. Her training got the best of her. *The perfect butler always rises to the occasion.*

She said, "I'm sure Q can spare seven of the cardboard oblongs he has for oversize sheet-cakes."

"Danner, you're invaluable." Elli beamed.

"We'll get the cards and find a marker," the twins said, racing away to the kitchen.

"I'll find Third," Elli said, hurrying offstage.

Alone at center stage, Mallory pointed her forefinger to her head like a gun and mentally quoted Hamlet, *To be, or not to be: that is the question.*

Knowing there was no choice for her, she lowered her handgun and marched to the dressing room.

WEST STOOD in the middle of the ballroom, searching the crowd for Mallory, wondering why he couldn't work up any interest in the four women who surrounded him.

They were all acquaintances from his past, socialites he had wooed and won. There had been no commitments, no hard feelings and no broken hearts. He had long ago perfected the delicate art of conducting and concluding his brief liaisons with tact, courtesy, humor and discretion.

Looking from one to the other of his admirers, West tried to recall what had once attracted him to each of them.

Whatever it had been, they held no appeal for him now. Somehow Renee, Samantha, Jillian and Drew just didn't measure up any longer. They seemed so...alike.

Beakins was making points with them by quoting an old Billy Crystal line. "You look mahvelous!"

West saw his aunt coming toward him through the crowd, waving her wand to catch his attention. "Excuse me, ladies. Aunt has reserved the next dance with me."

"Third," Elli said breathlessly when he met up with her. "Come backstage. Danner and I need you."

Mahvelous. He'd been wondering where Mallory was. Now he'd find out. Interested to no end, he escorted Elli across the ballroom and through the stage curtains.

"Okay," he said. "What's the problem?"

Elli explained the situation, adding, "I just hope the prince's tights and doublet fit you."

"Does he get to kiss Cinderella?"

"Why, yes." She smiled. "At the end."

"I can hardly wait, Aunt."

"I knew you'd rise to the occasion, Prince."

"Lead me to my tights."

"Tight squeeze!" warned Beakins.

At the door of the dressing room, Elli knocked. "Are you changed, Danner?"

"My back zipper is stuck," Mallory responded. "Help!"

"You've got it," West said, walking right in.

His tongue almost stuck to the roof of his mouth when he saw her dressed in a frothy white tulle ball gown with a hoop skirt and décolleté neckline. Blanching, she clutched the bodice against her breasts.

"I meant Mrs. C.'s help."

"Aunt's arthritis is acting up. In her fingers."

He approached Mallory almost reverently. She was the loveliest creature he'd ever seen. In the mirror behind her, he could see her bare back where the zipper gaped open to her waist. Bare, creamy, flawless skin.

"I'll go powder my nose," Elli said, disappearing.

West took in a deep breath and let it out slowly. "You look beautiful, Angel."

"Thank you." She backed up against the mirror and her hoops billowed forward.

West perched Beakins on a clothes rack. "Turn around. I'll help you."

As he came to her, she hesitated. Then she closed her eyes and pivoted, saying, "It's caught . . . at the waist."

"Mmm-hmm." He looked into the mirror and saw her pulse leaping wildly in the hollow of her throat. Taking the zipper tab between his finger and thumb, he said, "Arch your back away from me a little. A little more."

"I was being so careful," she murmured, "and then it stuck. Everything's gone wrong all at once."

"Everything's going right, now," he said, working the zipper free and slowly raising it to the top. "We're going to be a big hit together." He watched her eyelids flutter open as he placed his hands on her upper arms. "Did I tell you you're all I thought about while I was gone?"

"West—"

"If I didn't, I'm telling you now. You were on my mind. Was I on yours?"

She nodded. "Most of the time."

Meeting her gaze in the mirror, he curled his fingers around her warm, creamy flesh. She still had her hands crossed over the top of her breasts. What was she hiding?

"Angel—" He broke off, speechless, as she dropped her hands to her sides.

She said softly, "You'd better get changed."

"I'm not sure I can even breathe," he replied in a strained whisper, his gaze drawn to the swell of her breasts above the low neckline of the gown.

The bodice was a size too small and the push-up effect was stunning, breathtaking. He had the immediate thought that every man at the ball would be passionately in love with her the moment the curtain rose.

Realizing how many men's eyes would soon devour her, West felt an instant flash of blind fury toward every male in the ballroom.

She's mine, damn it! he found himself thinking fiercely. *Mine!*

"Love hurts!" squawked Beakins.

Startled by the bird, West became aware that his hands were clenching Mallory's arms in a bruising grip. She was swaying back against him, making a muffled sound, as if he were causing her pain. As he loosened his hold, she turned around and swayed forward.

He took her into his arms, into a gentle, cherishing embrace. "I'm sorry. I didn't mean to hurt you."

"You didn't." Her arms slipped around his waist. She nestled her cheek against his chest.

"Angel, all of a sudden I—"

A rap sounded on the door. "Break a leg." Elli's voice. "Show must go on."

"Coming," Mallory called faintly, pulling away from West. She smoothed her skirts, pointed out his costume on the clothes rack, opened the door and let herself out.

Beakins lapsed into Spanish. *"¡Hasta la vista!"*

In a daze, West changed from his pirate outfit into royal-blue tights and a matching doublet with gold trim. Something had happened, but he wasn't sure what. Something he'd never experienced before.

Something heartfelt and tender, yet sensuous and erotic, all at once.

He came out of the dressing room feeling light-headed and confused. A dimwit Prince Charming, for sure.

As he came onstage, behind the closed curtains, West noticed that Mallory seemed to be surrounded by an aura. Almost as if she had descended on evanescent wings from the puffy white clouds in the blue silk sky. *Angel.* He felt half drunk, yet he hadn't had anything to drink.

Ensconced on the fairy throne, his aunt pointed out his stage marks to him with her wand and introduced the jesters. They showed him the cue cards they'd made. West nodded that he understood, which he did . . . sort of. He was supposed to act enchanted, like a dunderhead in an altered state. Well, looking at Cinderella he wouldn't have to act.

And he couldn't forget that he'd get to kiss her.

"Take your marks," Tom—or Tim—said from stage left. He stuck one hand through the curtain, a cue to the orchestra, which began playing a fanfare of "Some Enchanted Evening." The music segued into a drumroll as the jesters parted the curtains and pulled them open. The ballroom hushed, cymbals crashed and the twins somersaulted to front stage center.

"Ladies and gentlemen!" they announced together. "The Silly Season Players present a simply silly show. The place—the silliest kingdom ever. The time—ten minutes to midnight. The players—Fairy Godmother, Cinderella and Prince Charming. We two are Nit and Wit."

The silliness commenced according to the revised situation.

Godmother to jesters. "Nit and Wit you are, indeed. Both present, but not accounted for.

Nit/Wit look overjoyed, as if praised. Do back flips, cartwheels, somersaults.

Godmother to audience. "Such is also the case with Prince and Cindy here. Present, but not accounting for the love spell I've cast on them. A short circuit in my wand, I fear. Cindy, don't you feel the least bit different?"

Cindy—ditzy. "Gee, Godmother, I dunno. Is Prince what I had in mind when I wished upon a star?"

Godmother—dryly. "In mind? A mind is precisely what you lack, Cindy."

Cindy—blinks, smiles. "Oh. Right."

The audience chuckled.

Godmother. "And you, Prince. What have you to say for yourself?"

Prince. "Huh?"

Godmother. "Nit! Trot out Prince's first line, please."

Nit holds up cue card.

Prince. "Wanna have sex with me, Cindy?"

The audience laughed.

Cindy—dumb smile. "Okay."

More laughter from the audience.

Godmother. "No, no, no, Prince. Wit, point out each word for him. Slowly."

Prince—slowly. "Wanna have sex—"

Godmother—incensed. "Prince! Repeat after me. Will you have the *next* dance with me, Cinderella?"

Cindy—dumb smile. "Okay."

Godmother—wearily, to her wand. "Where did we go wrong? Is it you? Is it me? Or is romance simply not what it used to be? Are young men and women not at all what they used to be?"

Jesters tumble and clown around like the Three Stooges, trying to cheer her up.

Godmother—uncheered. "I long for the days of old when poetry reigned and romance filled the air. When love budded and bloomed before you-know-what got into the act."

Cindy. "What, Godmother?"

Godmother. "S-e-x."

Prince—responds with loud wolf whistle.

Godmother to audience. "You see what it's come to nowadays. No blushing lovers. No enchanted evenings. No magic." *Checks her wristwatch.* "Drat! Two minutes to the stroke of midnight, and still no love spell transforming these two."

THE SILLY SHOW might have gone on to its silly conclusion if Beakins hadn't gotten into the act just then. Croaking "Step this way! Make my day!" he strutted onto the stage.

The audience roared.

Quick-witted Elli improvised the next line. "Hark! It's Beak the Sorcerer, in disguise. He's the villain blocking my spell, I'll bet."

The jesters rushed to scoop the sorcerer up, but he fluttered out of their grasp and took refuge under Cindy's hoop skirt. She lifted it a few inches, but the sorcerer was nowhere to be seen.

He could only be heard. "Foxy lady!"

"I'll get him," declared Prince with a gleeful gleam in his eyes. He dove straight as an arrow to the floor of the stage and slid on his belly halfway under Cindy's skirt.

"Godmother!" she exclaimed, looking shocked and appalled as Prince and the sorcerer scuffled around and between her legs. "He's—eek!—climbing up my—er—pantaloons!"

Prince, visible only from waist to feet, was wriggling his hips and kicking his heels in the air as he groped to halt Beak's ascent.

Cindy began jiggling her skirt and hopping as if she had ants in her pantaloons. A few downy scarlet feathers puffed out from under her hoop and floated up to the blue silk sky as Beak the Sorcerer led Prince on a merry chase down under.

On the throne, Godmother was laughing hysterically. Nit and Wit were having fits, holding their splitting sides. The guests were almost rolling on the ballroom floor.

"Yeeeeeek!" screamed Cinderella, jumping a foot into the air with her legs spread-eagled.

"Gotcha!" Prince exulted, emerging with the Sorcerer clutched in both hands.

"Le' go my Eggo!" the villain protested.

"Release us from your wicked spell first," Prince demanded, rising to his feet.

"Allow *me*," said Godmother, "to dispel his spell." Shaking with laughter, she came down from her throne and touched her wand to the sorcerer's bedraggled blue tail feathers.

As if vanquished, the bird struggled out of Prince's hold and perched upon Godmother's shoulder.

As if bewitched, Prince turned to Cindy, went down on one knee and extended one hand.

As if charmed, the audience quieted and leaned toward the stage. An expectant hush fell over the ballroom like a magic spell.

As if enthralled, Cinderella smoothed her skirt, straightened into a regal posture and placed her hand in Prince's.

"May I have the honor of this dance, Cinderella?"

"I am honored to accept, Prince Charming."

The band struck up the "Cinderella Waltz" and Prince Charming whirled Cinderella around the stage, under the puffy clouds and the sparkling stars and the iridescent rainbows. He waltzed her to center stage, gathered her into both arms and gazed down into her eyes.

Cinderella looked up at him and then melted into his embrace, into his kiss, into happily ever after.

The music soared to an end as the jesters slowly brought the curtains closed. Godmother sighed with enormous satisfaction at the fairy tale she had made come true.

She checked her watch. It was the stroke of midnight, on the dot. Hearing her guests break into waves of applause beyond the closed curtains, she signaled Nit and Wit to open them again for a curtain call.

Not that Prince Charming and Cinderella were aware of anything but each other, she noted. They were still locked in a kiss, too enchanted by magic to pull apart, too spellbound to take a bow.

Godmother smiled secretively as she took a bow with Nit, Wit and Beak the Sorcerer. She was thinking how very wise she had been to pay two Silly Season players to stay out of the play tonight.

Very wise, indeed!

8

EXCEPT FOR the waltz and the almost endless kiss, Mallory was hazy on the details once the curtain descended. After somehow parting her lips from West's and changing into her tuxedo, she was back on the job. Concentrating wasn't easy.

She would never forget being an enchanted princess in the arms of the handsomest prince in the kingdom. Nonetheless, she mustn't forget that she was the butler again. Not Cinderella at the ball.

"More champagne?" she murmured, passing among the guests with an almost empty bottle of Veuve Clicquot. Coffee and light sandwiches were being served to fortify the guests for their trip home.

"Hey," she heard a man near her say. "Fill 'er up over here, Cindyrella." He was about West's age, brawny, imposing and opulently costumed as King Henry VIII. And, she observed, he was much the worse for drink. Too bad. He'd been as charming as a teddy bear when she'd announced his arrival earlier.

"I'll uncork a fresh bottle," she told him. "A king of England should have more than dregs."

"Rrrrright-o, wench," he agreed, giving her right rear a lascivious pinch. "You come back now, y' hearrrr?"

"Oh, I'll be back."

Never letting on that she'd felt the pinch, she took up a fresh bottle and went to Ellinor, who was sitting out a dance. Pretending to request Elli's approval of wine, she leaned down next to her and whispered in her ear.

"Mr. Livingstone Carmichael has been overserved. He's becoming a nuisance."

Elli frowned. "Stone Carmichael. One of Third's old college friends, I think."

"That's right. Shall I handle the situation?"

"Right away," said Elli. "Have you seen Third?"

"No. Not since . . . backstage."

"You were both marvelous up there."

"Thank you, Mrs. C. I'll tend to Mr. Carmichael." Mallory hurried away, her cheeks hot. "Marvelous" didn't begin to describe Prince Charming.

Luckily she didn't have time to dwell on her most recent memories of West. She had a drunken guest to quietly remove from the ballroom. She knew just how to do it. But when she returned to Carmichael, she found West—dressed as a pirate again—confronting him.

"I saw that, Stone," West was saying.

"Saw what?" said Livingstone, swaying unsteadily.

"Everything. You're on your way out right now." West gripped Stone's burly arm. "Nobody pinches Angel, pal."

"Excuse me, Mr. Cade," Mallory intervened, seeing that West looked ferocious. She made her tone as formal as possible. "Mr. Carmichael has a phone call in the library."

Carmichael's eyes bugged out. "H'ray, it's the serving wench." He waved his empty glass. "Fill 'er up."

West stepped in between them. "Stone, maybe you didn't hear what I just—"

Mallory cut in, giving West a sharp look, "The caller says it's *extremely* important. If your guest will come to the telephone, I'll serve him a drink there."

"Yeah," Carmichael rejoined, "she'll serrrrve me whereverrr..."

West warned, "I'll be right behind you, Stone. Watch your step—and your pinchers."

Relieved for the moment, Mallory turned and led the way to the library. West was complicating the problem and making her job more difficult. He had almost caused an unnecessary scene. But recognizing his motives sent another rush of heat to her cheeks.

He had defended her honor and offered his protection. Just like a chivalrous prince in the days of old. To her complete surprise, she found it thrilling to be defended and protected.

Inside the library, she stayed proper, stiff and inscrutable. Stepping between the door and the two men, she said, "I'm sorry, Mr. Carmichael, but there is no call for you. Mrs. Cade feels we've been remiss in serving you too much wine tonight. She requests that you relax in the library until you wish to return home."

West moved to her side and linked arms with her. "All right," he conceded in a low, admiring tone. "You handle him and I'll watch."

"Would you prefer some coffee, Mr. Carmichael?"

"Hell, no!" he thundered belligerently. "I'll leave now!"

West started to say something, but Mallory stopped him with another sharp look. She held out a hand to

Carmichael. "Please provide me your car keys, sir, and I'll bring your car around myself."

"Tha's more like it, wench." He dug in his waistcoat and tossed his keys at her feet.

West bent and picked them up, murder in his eyes. "If you weren't drunk to the eyeballs, I'd—"

Mallory broke in, "Give me the keys, West."

"You're going to get his car, Angel? Are you crazy?"

"West, I've done this many times before."

West shrugged, then reluctantly gave her the keys. "I'll keep him from going anywhere." Crossing his arms over his chest, he turned back to his old college friend and said with exaggerated politeness, "Have a seat, Stone. Make yourself comfortable."

Mallory slipped out and immediately called a taxicab. It arrived within five minutes, time for her to determine Carmichael's home address from the guest list. Reentering the library, she found him ranting at West. West looked ready to punch him in the nose.

"Your cab is here to take you home, sir," she announced. "The driver has been paid and tipped. I'll have your car delivered to you tomorrow morning."

"And I'll show you out, buddy," West said, hauling him to his feet.

"The cab is waiting at the side door," Mallory told him. "No one will see or know."

West nodded approvingly as he muscled Carmichael out of the library. "You think of everything, Angel. Thank God."

Grateful for West's superior strength, Mallory followed behind them and breathed a sigh of relief. A guest the size of a defensive linebacker would have been

impossible for her to restrain if he had insisted on par-
tying all night. With West applying the force, Carmichael had no say in the matter.

However, that didn't keep him from berating West
all the way outside and then inquiring, "What's your
beef, loverrrboy? 'S she *your* wench?"

"She's a lady," West said menacingly, "and you owe
the lady an apology."

"Pay him no attention, West," Mallory told him,
trying to reason.

"Loverrrboy's lady, huh?" Carmichael mocked.
"Jusht a hot number, like all the other numberrrs you
scr—"

West cut him off. "Get in the cab."

Mallory held the taxi door open for West to stuff him
into the back seat. "Good night, Mr. Carmichael."

Carmichael had the last word. "'Night, wench."

Mallory slammed the cab door shut just as West
raised a fist at him. The cabdriver honked and took off.

"Jackass bastard," West muttered. "Pardon my
français. Hard to believe I used to like Stone in college.
He never could hold his liquor."

Looking at Mallory, West had an urge to take her in
his arms as he'd done earlier in the dressing room and
on the stage. He felt compelled to sweep her up and
carry her away somewhere, where he could make love
to her and possess her and make her his alone.

Having never desired a woman in that multitude of
ways before, he didn't understand his emotions now.
He'd never gone into a rage over anyone's drunken
ravings.

"We'd best go in," Mallory was saying. She turned toward the door. "Thank you for your help."

"No problem, Angel." He followed her inside.

A primitive male rage simmered to a boil in him again as he viewed Mallory from behind and remembered Stone palming her bottom and calling her a wench. Balling his hands into fists, he wished that he'd given Stone two big, fat lips.

MALLORY COULDN'T sleep after the ball ended. The cleanup crew had done a quick, efficient job under the housekeeper's direct supervision, so there was little left for anyone to do or to worry about. The house was still and silent, it was two a.m. and Mallory couldn't sleep.

She could only think of West. The waltz. The kiss. What a surprise his chivalry had been.

He had gone the whole evening without pairing up with a woman. He had led the first dance with Ellinor, then hadn't danced with anyone else but Cinderella. What's more, he had waltzed beautifully, proof that he had faked needing dance instruction last week. Endearing proof.

Mallory thought back to the lesson, to the fantasy and intimacy she had shared with him, to the sensations and emotions he had aroused in her. Sexual sensations. Emphatic emotions. Fantasies without end.

Restless and sleepless, she got out of bed. Maybe some fresh air would cool her off and clear her mind.

TOO WIRED to sleep after the ball was over, West opened his bedroom window and leaned out to breathe the night air. The moon was almost full, lighting the terrace fountain behind the house. Water sprayed up in shimmering arcs, then rained down into the circular, moonlit pool.

He could clearly see someone in one of the chaise lounges arranged around the fountain. A woman in profile, lost in thought.

Angel! He threw on his pajama bottoms, slid down the banister and went out to join her.

Tiptoeing onto the flagstone terrace behind her, he noted that her hair fell loose and curly to her shoulders. Wrapped in a white terry-cloth robe, she looked luminous and ethereal, as if she had bathed in moonbeams. He cleared his throat to announce his presence.

She started and turned. "Oh. West . . . hello."

"Can't sleep worth a damn," he said, dropping down on the double chaise next to her. "You, too?"

She nodded. "It was quite a night."

"You did quite a job. Everything perfect. Not a hitch. I told Aunt to give you a bonus and she told me she'd already made out a check."

She gazed ahead at the fountain and smiled. "I'll have to splurge on something."

West studied her profile, reflecting on everything he'd learned about her so far. He realized that he had begun to admire her brisk efficiency and the dedication she brought to her work. It had paid off tonight. But she was too serious most of the time. She'd probably splurge on nothing more than a new bow-tie blouse. What fun a man could have pampering her with luxuries and special treats.

"Look at Goldfinger and Moneypenny," she said.

West glanced over and saw the two cats lapping water from the edge of the pool. They drank, then chased each other into a nearby hedge. Focusing again on Mallory, West felt a powerful urge to shower her with glittering jewels, bowers of flowers and castles in Spain.

Mallory felt his gaze on her and her blood warmed. She thought of all the women West could have been with tonight, all the women he'd had in the past. Yet he was alone after the ball. Maybe he'd spent his essential energies during his trip. Maybe not. He didn't look spent.

Hearing a mewling sound beyond the hedge, she turned slightly toward it. "Listen. Is that a baby crying?"

"Sounds like caterwauling cats to me," West said. "Moneypenny begging Goldfinger to make kittens with her."

Mallory cocked her ear as the mewl rose to a plaintive wail and died away.

West reached over and took her hand. "Hey, pay some attention to your hot date here."

"You're my employer's nephew, not my date." She was making only a token resistance. She didn't pull her hand out of his. His touch was already making her weak, spurring desire.

West tilted her chin with his other hand, mounting a token argument. "You're my aunt's butler, not mine. We could date. People do it all the time. When's your next night off?"

"I'm free right now."

Mallory didn't turn away from the soft kiss he placed on her lips. She didn't make herself get up and leave. She lingered there, letting West have his way.

She put all the no's out of her mind. Why should it matter that West was bare to the waist, only wearing pajama bottoms? It didn't. Tonight she was brimming with urges to say yes to everything she wanted. West was welcome to tempt her into misbehaving again.

"Live in the moment," he murmured. He rose to his feet, drawing her up with him into his embrace, where he kissed her again. "It's not such a big sin, Angel. Why don't you try it?"

She nodded, willing to let herself go with him.

"Come right this way. Forget past and future." He led her by the hand to the pool around the fountain and stepped into the knee-deep water. "Have fun. Get your feet wet."

She dipped a toe into the pool and giggled

He kicked up a tiny splash and grinned. "Be. Here. Now. With me."

He was the strongest temptation in the world. Mallory set one foot in the pool. West backed through the water toward the falling spray. She stepped right in with him.

Giving her a soulful, half-lidded gaze, he puckered his lips and kissed the air in front of them. Irresistible. On a sudden whim, she splashed him. He began splashing back.

It was so childish. So playful. So much fun!

Soon they were both beneath the spray, chortling under their breath, drenching each other in a water fight. Her absorbent terry robe got waterlogged and weighed her down. West's pajama bottoms became plastered to his skin.

Soaked and clinging to each other for balance, they romped and cavorted. Then, slowly, their mood sobered and softened. Breathless laughter became breathless anticipation. They stood embracing, blinking droplets of water out of their eyes, becoming lost in each other.

"Having fun, Angel?"

"Yes."

"There's more in store," he murmured, loosening the tie around her waist.

"Oh, yes . . ." He was so appealing, so alluring. Tracing her fingers over the pattern of wet hair on his chest, Mallory leaned back and invited him to part the lapels of her robe. She wanted to feel his skin against hers. She wanted to keep on and on, having the time of her life.

Pressing her bare breasts against him, she rose into his kiss and twined her arms around his neck. He kissed her until they both almost toppled. Then he lifted her into his arms and carried her out of the pool to the double chaise.

He set her on it and stretched out beside her, kissing her again and opening her robe all the way down the front. "Tell me I'm dreaming and I'll believe it, Angel."

It *was* like a dream, Mallory thought as West's hand cupped the curve of her breast. An erotic dream in which moonlight bathed her body, revealing shadowed secrets to her passionate lover. His mouth was leaving hers and moving down to where he cupped her in his palm, where his thumb was circling her nipple.

She curled her nails into his muscled shoulders as his lips teased the peak of her breast. His teeth nibbled, his tongue twirled, his breath whispered back and forth from tip to tip.

Soon she was gasping, panting his name and touching the pleasure points on his chest with fervent fingertips. He flung his head up and howled softly at the moon. Then he looked down into her eyes and slipped his hand between her thighs.

"Since we aren't . . . protected," he murmured, "I'll be . . . creative. Okay?"

As his fingers drifted upward, Mallory caught her breath. She had spun so far out of control that she hadn't thought of responsibilities and consequences. West, of all people, was the one thinking ahead.

"West, I'm not—I mean, you—"

"Sshhh. Just relax and be yourself."

"But I'm not—"

"I'll protect you, Angel." He laid a fingertip on her lips and caressed her breasts with his mouth again. He sucked the taut crests to pearl-hard peaks.

"Doesn't it all feel good?" he whispered. "In all the right places?"

"Oh, yes." She could hardly breathe, it felt so good. "But . . ."

"It's going to feel better and better. Believe me."

The gentle, coaxing way he was touching her made it impossible to disbelieve him. Her thighs were weakening, parting and quivering as his stroking fingers neared their goal. He flexed his hips against the side of her thigh, and she could feel how fully aroused he was.

Closing her eyes, she heard his breath shudder deep in his throat when he made the first intimate contact. She felt his hammering heart shake his body.

His whisper trembled in her ear. "Look at me, Angel. Let me see how I make you feel."

She opened her eyes and saw a rapt, almost reverent expression on his face and in his heavy-lidded gaze. He appeared to want her greatest pleasure more than anything in the world.

She couldn't help wanting it, too. His slow, sinuous, deepening caress was filling her with runaway desire, making her feel reckless, fiery and ready to explode.

Abandoning all restraint, her hips undulating faster and faster, she clung to West's shoulders. She didn't hold back the whimpers and sighs of her approaching ecstasy. Closer and closer, higher and higher.

On the brink of discovering where he was taking her, she heard a baby cry. Louder and louder, only a few feet away. Time seemed to stand still. She tensed, stopped moving, and the cry rose to a wail. A distress signal.

"What the hell?" West said, holding still to listen.

"It's a baby," she told him thickly. "Not cats."

He burrowed his face in her hair and half groaned. "Not now. Why now?"

The wail didn't trail away and stop this time. It rose into the night air, a human, heartrending sound.

West sighed. "You may be right. But . . . a baby?"

"It's very close," she said, easing out of West's arms. "Just beyond the hedge."

"Yeah. Too close for comfort. Just when you were almost—"

"We should go look, West."

"Okay. Let's go."

Mallory closed her sopping wet robe around her and cinched the tie.

In a wry tone, West said, "If all we find is cats in heat, I told you so."

Mallory slipped with him through a break in the hedge, certain that they wouldn't find cats mating. After all, the four Cade cats had been neutered. She followed the sound of the plaintive cry.

It led straight to a baby in a basket.

9

"WEST, it *is* a baby!"

The crying stopped the instant Mallory and West knelt next to the basket. The moonlight was so bright that the large print on the note pinned to the baby's blanket could be read: Have a heart. She's Valentine. Six months old.

"Valentine," he said wonderingly. "She's not crying anymore. She's sort of . . . smiling."

Mallory and West huddled over the basket together. Her heart melted a little as a tiny hand emerged from under the pink blanket and grasped her forefinger.

"A sweet, innocent, abandoned baby," she murmured.

West nodded. "Wonder whose it is."

"Dah-dah-dee," Valentine babbled, looking at West.

"Hey, Angel. She called me Daddy."

Mallory's heart lurched. "Maybe she's—yours?"

"No way," he immediately protested. "Not me. Uh-uh. Call me irresponsible, *except* when it comes to safe sex and birth control." He paused, searching her expression for belief. "I've always used the best protection. Always."

"Whatever the case, West—"

"The case," he cut in, growing agitated, "isn't what you think. I haven't done anything to be accused of fatherhood."

"I'm not accusing you."

"You're not believing me, either. You're letting my reputation get in the way of the truth. Was I careless for even one second tonight with you?"

"We'd better take Valentine inside and argue later," she said.

He moved to pick up the basket, but Mallory held him back a moment.

"West, I don't want you to take further offense, but news of an abandoned baby found in this particular backyard is going to raise some very sticky questions. They'll be directed at you."

He considered her words, then said, "You're right. The press will be swarming all over the place. They're great at making something out of nothing."

Mallory nodded, thinking. "We should be careful not to wake anyone but Mrs. C. when we go inside. For obvious reasons, the staff shouldn't know that you and I were out here together. Mrs. C. might understand how this all happened, but . . ."

"She'll understand, Angel. And she'll never give away our secret. I know her."

"Even so, if we could both dry off and change clothes before we tell her we've found a baby, that would help."

"If we do that," he mused, "then we'd say we both heard the crying and came out at the same time to investigate?"

"It's worth a try, West."

"Maybe not, Angel. Valentine might get loud again when we get inside. It might wake up the cooks or the maids. They'd barge out of their rooms and catch us looking like this."

Mallory said, "I'd never live it down with the staff."

"Here's what we'll do," West said decisively. "You go inside alone right now and start changing your clothes and drying your hair."

"What about you?"

"In a few minutes, I'll take Valentine inside with me. If she cries and wakes anyone besides Aunt, I'll say I was out in the fountain splashing around when she cried and I found her. Aunt will naturally call you to help."

"But what reason will you make up for splashing around alone in a knee-deep fountain?"

"Too much champagne at the ball."

"That's logical," she agreed slowly. "You'll take Valentine to Mrs. C.'s suite and then you'll ring me to come help. I'll pretend it's the first I've heard of it."

"Right. Perfect."

Mallory handed the basket to West. "Don't drop her."

"I won't. Cute little squirt, isn't she?"

"Yes. I'll go inside now."

Mallory turned and walked toward the house. To her dismay, she saw the back door open. Elli came out, wearing a long silk dressing gown.

"Danner, there you are. Did you hear a baby cry, too?"

"Er, uh—" Mallory gulped and began shivering in her soaked robe. "Well, yes, I—um—came out here to see—"

"At first I thought it was Moneypenny or one of the other cats," Elli broke in as she reached where Mallory had halted, "but then I had second thoughts. Oh, is that Third over there by the fountain?"

"Uh, yes, he heard—too."

"And what does he have there?"

Mallory swallowed hard. "A basket. I was just going inside to—" She stopped, seeing West coming forward to where she stood with Elli.

"Aunt," he said, "we were on our way in to wake you up. Look what we found by the box hedge."

Valentine babbled, "Dah-dah-dah-dee."

"A baby!" Elli exclaimed. "Oh, let me see."

West lowered the basket for her to look inside. "Valentine—that's her name—seems to be abandoned, Aunt. She's not very old. Six months."

"What a sweet, darling name. Valentine. Look at those big wide eyes and apple cheeks. And she's got red hair. Precious little girl." She glanced up from the baby at West and Mallory. "You look drenched, both of you."

West cleared his throat. "I was showing Angel how the fountain works. And she tripped. And fell in. And then I jumped in to . . . you know . . . and we got pretty soaked."

"Letting off steam together, in other words," Elli concluded shrewdly. "I quite understand."

"See? No problem," West said to Mallory.

Elli focused again on the baby. "Well, Valentine. Shall we take you inside and decide what to do with you?"

"Aunt, let's take her in *quietly*, okay?"

"*Very* quietly," she agreed. "The staff shouldn't know anything about this until tomorrow. We'll explain then that you were out here alone and heard the baby and summoned Danner to help you."

Mallory let out the breath she'd been holding.

"Everyone inside," said Elli, leading the way to the house. "Let Valentine suck on your finger, Third, so she won't cry and wake up the neighborhood."

They went into the house, up to Elli's suite, where she continued in command. "Third, you and Danner go dry off and change clothes. I'll get acquainted with Valentine in the meantime. Then we'll make some decisions."

Mallory went to her suite to change into slacks and a sweater and blow-dry her hair. West did the same.

He returned to his aunt's quarters first and got orders from her to go up to the north attic. "I have a set of baby things stored there," she told him, her eyes misting. "In the smallest cedar chest, for the baby I lost."

West took her into his arms and held her to comfort her. "Maybe it's not good for you to open old wounds, Aunt."

"I think they've finally healed, Third. Please get the chest and bring it here. There's a cradle, too, stored in the largest steamer trunk."

He moved to go, but she stopped him for a moment. "Third, I have to ask you a very personal question and you have to tell me the truth." She turned from him to the baby basket. "Did one of your wild oats result in this child?"

"I swear to God, Aunt, I've never sown any. I always used my own protection to make sure. It never failed me."

"I believe you," Elli said, "but seeing that Valentine has red hair and blue eyes just like Michelle's, I couldn't help but wonder if you'd played a part."

West shook his head. "I never touched Michelle. You told me hands off, remember?"

"Yes. Thank you for keeping your word to me. Now, hurry to the attic. Valentine needs a dry diaper."

Mallory came in as West was leaving. "I'll be back in a flash," he told her. "Hold down the fort."

She watched him stride away down the hall, then entered Elli's parlor. "I'm back, Mrs. C."

After explaining where West had gone, Elli said, "I'm very relieved that Third isn't Valentine's father. He swears it, and I believe him. I hope you will, too."

"I don't have any reason to doubt his word," Mallory said.

"His reputation is enough to make anyone doubt, Danner. Also, Valentine has many features in common with my former maid, Michelle. Red hair, blue eyes, fair skin. I had a sinking feeling until he swore to me that he wasn't the man."

Mallory privately wondered how many redheads he had bedded fifteen months ago.

"He says he's always been extra careful," Elli went on after a moment of reflection. "Not that the police will believe that when we report Valentine to them. The publicity will be very nasty."

Mallory nodded, already picturing the headlines and the TV news. There would have to be denials and blood tests.

Elli sighed. "Our trust and support may be all Third can rely on when the news hits the fan. May I count on you to believe him as I believe him?"

"I'll never speak a word to the contrary, Mrs. C."

"Danner, that isn't the same as believing him. Has he made you mistrust him for any reason?"

"No, Mrs. C."

Elli smiled and nodded. "I didn't think so. He *is* turning over a new leaf, isn't he? Aside from luring you into the fountain a while ago. I saw him from my window."

"You—" Mallory gulped "—saw?"

"Purely by accident. I happened to peek out at the moon right then. You both waded in and I shut the shade. I was happy to see him with you instead of that harem at the ball. Four lovely girls, but not right for Third."

Valentine babbled just then, and Elli took her up out of the basket. "Look what I found," she said. "Two full baby bottles are tucked in the blanket. We can warm one in my minimicrowave."

Shocked by thoughts of how much West's aunt might have observed, Mallory picked up one of the bottles, but stood rooted in place. An explanation was definitely called for, but how to explain?

"Mrs. C., I shouldn't have been out there with West. I should have come inside the moment he appeared on the terrace. Yet somehow I . . . stayed. I can't explain why, even to myself."

"I'm sure I know why," said Elli, cradling Valentine and crooning to her. "You were both still under Godmother's magic spell."

"Here's the chest," West announced, coming in with it. He set it by the basket. "I'll get the cradle."

"Wait a moment, Third." Elli looked at Mallory. "You've said you have triplet sisters you helped your father to raise. As the only child expert under this roof at the moment, would you be Valentine's temporary nanny until things are straightened out?"

"I'd be happy to, Mrs. C."

"Take the cradle to Danner's suite, then, Third."

"Whatever you say, Aunt." He left again.

Mallory went to Elli's efficient pantry and heated the bottle in the microwave. When she came back, Elli placed Valentine in her arms and then opened the chest. "Here it all is." She began drawing out a small layette.

Looking down into Valentine's soft blue eyes, Mallory remembered years of child care. Baby-sitting, potty training, washing diapers, cooking meals, holding down the fort with Dad.

Motherhood.

She knew firsthand what a heavy burden it had been, what a constant responsibility. Rocking Valentine in her arms, she felt old inner conflicts surfacing. Yet the child was eliciting maternal instincts, as well. Mallory couldn't help smiling down into its tiny, heart-shaped face.

Who, really, could resist this innocent, helpless, motherless Valentine? Looking up, Mallory saw West coming in the door.

"The cradle's in your room," he advised. "Now what?"

"Why don't you take Valentine and feed her a bottle," Mallory said, discomfited by her conflicting emotions. She put the baby in West's arms before he could protest.

Appearing taken aback, he asked, "What if she— breaks?"

"You're doing just fine," Mallory assured him as he sat down gingerly on Elli's sofa. She gave him the bottle. "Put it in her mouth. Yes, just like that."

When Valentine began sucking, a look of complete bafflement and surprise crossed his face. Then he gave the baby a goofy, delighted, endearing smile.

"Hey, Val," he murmured, cuddling her against his chest. "I think I'm getting the hang of it."

"Dah-dee-dah," burbled Val around the nipple. She reached up and clutched a handful of his chin.

"Oh, my God, I'm falling in love," West proclaimed, nipping on the tiny fingers with his lips.

"This baby looks so *much* like Michelle," Elli reflected, watching him. "And I'm sure she was pregnant when she quit. Maybe Valentine is hers and we shouldn't report this to the authorities right away."

"Maybe," Mallory half agreed, trying to think like a butler and not a foster mother. "On the other hand, Valentine could be anyone's child. She might have been kidnapped. We can't assume that she was abandoned by her birth parents. We should be notifiying the police right now."

"I think I can bully the chief into keeping the details top secret," West said.

"Bully?" Ellie questioned. "How?"

West winked at his aunt. "I happen to know the happily married chief has a mistress he keeps on Telegraph Hill. A word to the wise can work miracles."

Mallory realized that must have been how he'd kept Elli's mugging out of the news. Looking at West, seeing that he was an instant pushover for the baby, she felt the edges of her heart soften.

There was something about a man and a baby together, something almost more tender and protective than a woman and a baby together. The man's physical strength. The baby's physical helplessness. The human connection. The emotional equation.

Primal and appealing.

Eyes daft and dopey, West was crooning to Valentine as he held the bottle to her lips, acting just like a new father. He was showing the most unexpected side of himself that Mallory could imagine.

Father. She started seeing him in a sudden, new light, one that illuminated his deeper male qualities as well as his fun-loving nature.

Her thoughts surprised her by echoing the words West had spoken a few moments ago. *Oh, my God, I'm falling in love.*

He looked up at her right then and gave her a dazed smile that was full of wonder. "I didn't know babies were fun," he said.

Elli smiled at him. "Ah, the thrill of discovery. Bring her here for a diaper change."

"I'll get a warm washcloth," Mallory volunteered, heading to the bathroom.

West asked Elli, "Can I help, even though Val's a girl?"

When Mallory came out with the washcloth, she found West holding a soggy, disposable diaper between his thumb and forefinger. "Now what?" he asked helplessly.

"Into the bathroom wastebasket," Mallory instructed, handing the washcloth to Elli.

"Isn't Third precious?" Elli murmured after he went to dispose of the diaper. "He's giving every indication of being a fine father when his time comes. Soon, I hope, now that he's falling in love."

"Valentine is easy to fall in love with," Mallory murmured, handing Elli a cloth diaper from the layette.

"Something like that," said Elli, smiling. She applied the diaper and pinned it. "Third, where are you?"

"Washing my hands," he called from her bathroom.

"When you're finished, bring the little chest along with you to Danner's suite. She'll meet you there." Elli put Valentine into the basket and popped the warmed bottle into her mouth. "Off you go, Danner. I'll get dressed and presentable for the police. Third can call them from your phone extension."

As Mallory started downstairs with the baby, West caught up with her, carrying the chest.

"Hi, snookums," he whispered to Val. "Remember me? Dah-dee?"

Snookums. Mallory melted that much more and fell a little deeper in love with Westmoreland Cade III. She just couldn't help it. She almost groaned aloud. What was to become of her now?

FIFTEEN MINUTES after West called the chief of police— at the chief's mistress's apartment—a plainclothes detective arrived at the back door to investigate the mysterious case of the abandoned baby.

When the detective prepared to leave thirty minutes later with a full report for the chief's eyes only, baby Valentine remained in the secure, secret, temporary custody of Westmoreland and Ellinor Cade.

"No problem," the detective assured them and Mallory. "All you'll see in the papers or on the news is that a baby was found—and her description—but nothing about where she was found, or by whom, or whose custody she's in. Hundred percent guaranteed. The chief will keep you posted."

He took the basket, the note and the untouched bottle as evidence and left as quietly as he had arrived.

"Time for a few hours of sleep," Elli said to West and Mallory after the lieutenant had gone. "I'm beat." She withdrew and went upstairs.

Rocking the cradle in which Valentine had fallen asleep, West looked at Mallory. "I'll baby-sit. You get some rest."

"West, you can't stay here."

"No one'll ever know, Angel. You need some sleep." He settled more squarely in the armchair in her parlor. "Lock your bedroom door if you don't trust me. I'll be here when your alarm goes off."

"But you know nothing about babies. You have no—"

He cut her off with an adamant look and folded his arms over his chest. "We found Valentine together and we'll take care of her the same way. The first shift is mine. I'll wake you up if I can't cope."

"But—"

"Just pretend we're playing house."

Mallory saw that it would take a bomb to blast him out of the chair and away from Valentine's side. Overnight he had become fiercely parental and protective. Not that long ago he had been the World's Hottest Date, Prince of Pirates and Prince Charming. Now he was "Three Men and a Baby".

Too tired and mixed up by her emotions to argue with him, she went into her bedroom, closed the door and put on a flannel nightgown. She got into bed, set her alarm clock and turned out the lamp.

Almost instantly, she fell asleep.

DOZING in the armchair, West heard Mallory's alarm buzz. He opened his eyes and glanced down at the cradle. Valentine was sleeping peacefully, so sweet and innocent. He had never seen fingernails so tiny or skin so delicate and transparent. Her pink, rosebud mouth made a sucking motion as he watched her sleep.

Inordinate delight and tender concern welled up in him. He felt a compulsion to tuck her pink blanket more securely around her little form. He had never, ever had fun like this. No wonder people had babies. Bundles of fun.

Hearing Mallory's alarm turn off, he stretched his arms and yawned. He heard her brush her teeth in her bathroom and then he saw her door open.

Peeking out at him through the crack, she whispered, "How is she?"

"Super," he whispered back. "Come out and see."

As she opened the door a little wider he saw that she was wearing a nightgown. Ankle-length. High neck. Long sleeves. It shouldn't have had the instant effect of turning him on, but it did. He found himself wanting Mallory even more than he'd wanted her the night before. And in an entirely different way.

She whispered, "My robe is still wet. I don't have an extra one."

He covered his eyes with one hand to convey that he wouldn't look, but then he split his fingers a smidgen and cheated as Mallory tiptoed to the cradle.

"It's all right, I guess," she said, motioning him to lower his hand. "After last night, false modesty seems silly."

West gestured at Valentine. "Sweet dreams."

Mallory nodded and smiled, looking sleepy and vulnerable to West. Sexy. Sexier than any woman he had ever wanted. Lovely. Her hair framed her oval face in an enticing tangle of waves and curls. He could see her luscious breasts quiver gently beneath her gown.

He swallowed hard and held his hand out, palm up, to her over the cradle. "Come here, Angel. Sit in my lap."

Crossing her arms over her waist, she shook her head. "I'd better not."

He rose slightly and took her hand. "Please. I want to hold you."

"West . . ."

"I *have* to hold you. Here." He sat again, drawing her to him. "Right here."

Exhaling a long, quivering sigh, Mallory came to him. She couldn't resist the lambent glow in his eyes. It communicated so clearly that he needed her. She needed him, too. She had to feel his arms around her. Just one more time.

She sank onto his lap, meeting his lips with a deep, hot kiss. It felt too right to stop and think. She was falling in love with him, so much that it couldn't be denied or repressed any longer.

His breath became tremulous and so did hers. Sliding one hand into her hair and cradling her head as he kissed her, he slid his other hand up under her nightgown and caressed her breasts.

He nibbled her earlobe, slipped his exploring hand down into her panties. "I've got protection with me now. In my wallet."

"West, we shouldn't." Yet she shifted her thighs apart for him to touch her and she didn't get off his lap. She could feel him beneath her, overwhelmingly male and fully aroused.

"God, Angel, this is too much torture for either of us." He stood, cradling her in his arms. "Hold on. We're going to bed."

"Yes," she gasped.

West carried her into her bedroom to her four-poster with every expectation of being what he had always been in bed. In years on the loose, he had used, mastered and perfected every meaningless phrase and slick sexual technique under the sun. He knew just what to say and do, knew just when to say and do it.

A sophisticated bachelor who wanted to stay footloose and fancy-free had to be suave, glib, ambiguous. He had to be impossible for a woman to corner or pin down in thought, word or deed. Chase skirts; skirt involvements.

So West was stunned when years of experience started deserting him the moment he sank into Mallory's bed with her. He found himself fumbling with the buttons on her gown, and murmuring the most unconditional, unambiguous, unsophisticated words into her ear.

"I worship and adore you." He had never said anything that unequivocal to a lover in his life.

"How do these buttons work?" There had never been an item of female clothing he couldn't undo and remove in two seconds flat.

Yet he was all thumbs now, trying to get her undressed, dying to worship and adore her, telling her what a precious angel she was. *Precious.* A meaningful word he would never, ever have uttered between the sheets before.

Mallory startled him by lifting the hem of her gown up over her head in one smooth, graceful movement. She flung the garment away and turned to him, wearing only brief panties.

He gulped like a teenager, seeing her lush breasts sway invitingly with every move she made. "Angel, I'm—" he breathed deeply, loosing his cool "—speechless."

She didn't seem to be listening. She began running her hands beneath his crewneck sweater, helping him to take it off, laughing softly when he got it bunched around his neck in his haste and almost strangled himself.

Finally, thank God, it was off and he was able to feel her breasts against his chest. But then his fingers got knotted somehow in the elastic leg band of her panties. Frustration mounted again as he strove—and failed— to undress her completely.

Mallory was amazed to discover that Westmoreland Cade III was falling all over himself in her bed. He hadn't fumbled last night. Something had changed. He seemed extraordinarily excited, oddly impulsive and charmingly awkward. Rather than living up to his reputation, he seemed to have forgotten he had one.

With a rush of pleasure, she realized that West was acting like a man in love. Like her, he was out of control with emotion and desire. He was unsure of himself!

And that made him more irresistible to her than he had ever been, though he didn't seem to realize the effect he was having. He looked almost miserable.

"I'm sorry, Angel," he muttered ruefully. "I've gotten everything fouled up somehow. Nothing's happening the way it's supposed to."

"Yes, it is," she said, kissing his chest and boldly placing her hand against the zipper of his slacks to convince him. "I don't hear myself complaining. Do you?"

"No, but I can do better than this. A lot better."

Tossing modesty to the wind, she stroked his arousal through his trousers. "You feel like the best to me."

"I do?"

"Yes, you do."

"You're going to ruin me doing that, Angel."

Feeling reckless, she wiggled her panties down to her ankles and kicked them off. She even unbuttoned his waistband and lowered his zipper.

"Shall I save you from a slow death?" she lightly teased, toying with the elastic on his briefs.

He shook his head. "It wouldn't be slow the way I feel right now."

"I feel the same way," she said with a sigh.

"Angel . . ." He gathered her into his arms and said hesitantly, "I feel really different with you. Somehow, a kiss isn't just a kiss. I know it sounds idiotic, but . . ."

"No. It doesn't."

"I want you so badly that I'm not doing anything right. I should—"

She kissed his lips to stem his words. Not a simple kiss, but an open invitation. "It all feels right to me."

"Really, Angel?"

"Really, West."

Mallory was deeply touched by the vulnerable look in his eyes. She kissed him again and furrowed her fingers in his hair. He rolled her onto her back and took control.

Kneeling over her, he removed two condoms from his wallet and placed them within reach. Then he struggled to take off his slacks and briefs. For a precarious instant, he almost toppled over the side of the bed, but regained his balance and kicked off the last of his clothes.

"The last time I lose my finesse," he quipped self-consciously, lying down beside her. "I hope."

Mallory assured him, "You didn't lose interest." She grazed her fingers below his waist and curled them around him.

After that she couldn't say another word because West's eager mouth began devouring her breasts, sucking the peaks, expressing more interest in her than she had ever experienced.

She trembled with excitement when his tongue traced a circle around her navel. Clutching his shoulders, she could feel his powerful body trembling, too. His tongue glided lower, between her thighs, and parted her.

"Oh!"

She had never dreamed he'd do this the first time or that she'd so readily let him have his way. Her two lovers had shied away from erotic lovemaking, but West was leaving no doubt that this was an avid pleasure for him. His sleek, slippery tongue darted in and out, swirled around, discovered every nuance of her intimate secrets.

He didn't seem to want to stop. He seemed to want her to . . .

Giving a breathless moan, she shuddered and surged to climax. Ripples of ecstasy. Shivering, incoherent sighs. Exquisite, free-falling relief.

When she opened her eyes, West moved his hands from holding her hips to frame her face. He broke into a slow, sensual smile as his gaze searched hers.

"Good, Angel?"

She nodded dreamily. "My first time that way."

"You mean, no one ever . . . I mean, I'm the only one to ever . . . ?"

"Mmm-hmm." She touched her fingertips to his smiling lips. "You're the very first. Perfectly wonderful."

West felt so much pride and pleasure all at once that he almost thanked her. He felt supremely honored, as if she had given him a priceless gift.

"Everything seems like the first time for me, too," he said impulsively.

In all honesty, it did. There was a newness, a freshness he hadn't foreseen in making love to her. He had a special feeling he'd never had before, as if he'd begun to experience a renewal or a rebirth. Something unique was occurring and he sensed that he must cherish—and preserve—every moment of it.

Seeing Mallory reach for one of the packets he had set aside, he took it from her hand and posed a question he'd never had to ask before in bed. Another first.

"Angel, are you . . . well, untouched, otherwise?"

"No. I'm not a virgin."

"Because I wouldn't want to hurt you."

"I'm sure you won't."

She curled her fingers around his throbbing shaft and set up a gentle, rhythmic motion that made him sure he'd explode if he unclenched his teeth. Then with a light, trembling hand, she sheathed him in protection.

Poised between her thighs, he gazed into her gray eyes and suddenly became conscious that a vast difference existed between having sex and making love. He had never made the distinction before, but he was too far gone to know for certain whether his heart or his hormones were in charge.

Hormones, he halfheartedly lied to himself.

He moved against her, probed into her liquid heat and became one with her. Fighting for control, he felt her rotate her hips under him and welcome him deeper into her sleek, snug body. Her arms and legs wrapped around him in an embrace that made him feel like the most special man in the universe.

The more she gave, the more he wanted. And needed. He was spurred by a fierce, primitive desire to possess and keep her. She was making everything fresh and new for him. Harder and more urgent than ever in his life, he embedded himself deep inside her.

At the very deepest, he heard her gasp his name and felt her come to shuddering completion again. An instant later, his own explosive release wrung a hoarse, heartfelt groan from him.

Easing apart from Mallory after drifting down with her, West turned on his side and cushioned her back against his chest. He filled his hands with her sumptuous breasts and moving downward kissed each separate vertebra of her spine.

One thing was leading to another again, when Valentine started crying and broke the spell.

10

WEST CHANGED Valentine's diaper while Mallory took a quick shower and got dressed. It struck him that this must be much like being married: wife bathing; husband baby-sitting; baby kicking and cooing in the cradle.

He had never imagined anything like that for himself until long into the distant future. In Warren Beatty fashion, he'd thought of himself postponing marriage and children until time started running out. Yet here he was, getting the biggest kick out of it right now.

He felt ready to go out and conquer the world for his little "family." He told himself he was just having fun. Just playing house. Just pretending.

He hadn't been pretending in bed, though, which disturbed him. He had never felt more serious in his life than when he had made love with Mallory. Not love, he amended hastily. It hadn't been that. No. It had been . . .

The best!

On a purely sexual level, he'd move mountains and slay dragons to have her in bed with him again, but love had no place in a lover boy's life. Fun was the watchword. He was having the best fun ever and that was the extent of it.

"Isn't that right, Valentine," he said.

"Uh-uh," she grunted.

"Don't argue with Dah-dee," he admonished. "He wears the pants in this family. You wear the Pampers."

She burbled, "Dah-dee."

"That's my girl." He nodded approvingly and took her out of the cradle to look out the window. "There's a whole big world out there and Dah-dee has it on a string. Anything Valentine's heart desires, he can afford it. She wants a pony, no problem. She wants a Ferrari when she's eighteen, no sweat. Watch out for lover boys, though. They'll do anything to get into her Ferrari."

He remembered an encounter he'd once had in a Testarossa. Reflecting on his playful past usually brought a grin to his lips, but not this morning. He didn't want this little darling playing games in hot sports cars with lover boys. She might get her little heart broken. She might get used. She might get pregnant, for pete's sake. Men would be after her day and night, making Dah-dee furious. He was getting angry just thinking about it.

"West?"

Startled by Mallory's voice, he turned and saw her standing in the bedroom doorway. She was dressed in her gray wool butler suit. Bow-tie blouse. Black low-heeled pumps. A barrette held her glorious hair back at her nape.

"We'd better not let Val grow up," he found himself saying fervently.

"What?"

"Nothing. I mean, Val seems hungry. She's drool-ing."

"All babies drool," she said. "Here, let me hold her."

"No, I'll be the nanny today."

"West, there's more to child care than you think." Mallory was relieved to have the diversion of an argument. She hadn't known quite what to say to West otherwise.

Say that she loved him? No, he'd break and run. Announce that it had been her worst mistake to make love with him? True, but difficult to make him believe after having two shattering orgasms in his virile presence. Beg him to go away for good because she wouldn't be able to stay out of bed with him? Beyond the realm of possibility.

"I can learn about child care by doing it, Angel."

"Mrs. C. asked me to be the nanny, not you. You don't even know what to feed Val for breakfast, now do you?"

"Dah-dah-dee," babbled Val.

"See?" West challenged testily. "She's depending on me, not you. She didn't say Nah-nee, now did she?"

Mallory pursed her lips. "I'm beginning to believe that you're her real father. You may have fooled Mrs. C., but you can't fool everyone."

"Damn it, Angel, you're talking like a butler again."

"You don't need to swear at me, West."

He retorted, "You're refusing to believe me. Did we just use birth control or didn't we? Did I do anything to make you the least bit pregnant?"

"No, but I doubt that I'm the only woman you've slept with in the past fifteen months."

He didn't refute her logic. He just said, "I didn't sleep with Michelle. Get it through your head!"

"Stop shouting, West!"

"Why? You're shouting, too, just as loudly. What have I ever done to make you—"

"You've done more than any man I've ever known." Acutely, painfully conscious of how much she had fooled herself into fantasizing that he cared for her, she blurted, "Everyone knows you're a hot date!"

"That's not the news of the century," he scoffed. "So I've shown a talent for appreciating and enjoying many of the women I've met. It was a two-way street. So?"

Mallory fixed him with a scornful glare. "If one oat escaped out of thousands of encounters, it's no wonder."

Angry and growing more so, West repeated, "Thousands?"

Valentine began squalling. Mallory wished to do the same and vent her own dismay. Hot tears stung her eyes at the thought of what she had become.

She tossed her head. "Millions, for all I know. And now I'm one of them, damn you!"

West's hand shot out and gripped her arm. "You're different. You know you are."

"I only know I should never have made love with you. My father was right to fear that you'd seduce me."

His tone lowered and became terse. "You didn't stop me or yourself, Angel. You consented. You were willing. And you wanted what happened as much as I did."

"It can't happen again, West. I can't continue working here if it does. In fact, I see now that it would be best for me to resign immediately."

"Angel, don't—"

She pulled her arm out of his grip. "I'll give two weeks' notice right away. Take care of Valentine while I tell Mrs. C."

"What are you going to tell her?"

"The truth!" She went to the phone and rang Ellinor's suite. "Mrs. C., I must speak to you in absolute privacy. Now, if possible. No, Valentine is fine. Just exercising her lungs. Yes, that's what you're hearing in the background. Yes. I'll be right up."

She left West holding the wailing baby and hurried upstairs. Looking quizzical, Elli met her at the door and led her into the parlor of her suite.

"Danner, what is it?"

Mallory sat on the sofa Elli motioned her to and pulled herself together. "Mrs. C., I'm sorry to tell you that I've compromised my position as your butler. As a result, I've got to resign immediately, unless you want two weeks' notice."

"Compromised your position? How?"

"I've become...intimate...with your nephew." Mallory bowed her head. "I'm sorry."

"I don't see why, Danner." Elli raised her eyebrows. "What's the tragedy in that?"

Taken aback by the unexpected reply, Mallory struggled to make sense of it. "This is a serious matter. At the very least, it's unprofessional of me."

Elli waved a hand. "Love is no respecter of persons or professions. You've simply fallen head over heels, and I heartily approve. I don't want you to leave."

"The staff, Mrs. C. They'll lose their respect for my authority. It will carry no weight whatsoever."

"Does anyone know or suspect?"

"Not yet, but I've learned from experience that few secrets survive intact." Mallory couldn't forget her own ride down Vanessa's banister. It had been accidentally observed in its entirety.

"Am I right or wrong that you're in love with Third?"

Mallory sighed and her throat tightened. "Right. I expect it to wear off after I move on. He's not in love with me, naturally. He was just having fun."

"That remains to be seen," said Elli, looking thoughtful. "But you shouldn't continue here under circumstances that you feel are unfair. Maybe if Third goes away for a while, on a vacation or sales trip, you'll feel less pressure to make a snap decision."

"I'd just miss him and think about him, Mrs. C."

"It would give you time to sort out your feelings before quitting. Let me speak to him. I'll urge him to go off and sell an island or two. While he's gone, you can send out your résumé and see what comes of it."

"That would probably be best," Mallory conceded.

Elli gave her a fond smile. "If Third ever gives up following in Warren Beatty's footsteps, I'd be very pleased for you to be my niece-in-law."

"I'd be pleased, too, Mrs. C." The tears Mallory had been suppressing began to trickle out. "I didn't mean to fall in love with him. I've been so foolish."

"We're all fools for love, Danner. Let me get you a tissue." Elli's eyes brimmed with emotion. "And one for myself, too."

"THIRD, Danner gave me her resignation. She told me everything a half an hour ago."

West had Val in his lap and was holding a warm bottle of milk to her little rosebud mouth. Mallory had fixed the bottle and then told him that Elli wanted to speak with him.

"It just happened, Aunt. That's all I can say, except that I didn't do anything ungentlemanly."

"Do you understand her grave concerns?"

"Sure."

"And?"

"I've got concerns of my own."

Elli nodded knowingly. "Such as not falling in love, not getting married and not settling down."

"Yeah. More or less." He shrugged and tilted the bottle—the way Mallory had shown him—so that Valentine wouldn't swallow air bubbles.

"Danner is the marrying kind, Third. She's a much more serious, stable woman than the women you've had flings with until now."

"Too serious, Aunt. Angel should have more fun."

"Fun like you, in short."

"Sure. Oh, now and then she spreads her wings with me and flies. But she never just lets the good times roll."

"I agree with you in that sense," Elli said with a reluctant nod. "But fun isn't all there is to a fine life. I've told you many times—with no apparent result."

West shrugged again to make it appear that his aunt's words weren't hitting home. The whole situation was unprecedented and he'd already begun to think that he needed a long sales trip to straighten himself out. He was only thirty-four. There were plenty of years of fun ahead. He had to get back his old, frisky perspective on life.

Elli let out a loud, impatient sigh. "I want you to make yourself scarce for a while, Third."

"So do I, Aunt. I want to buy my own plane and hire a full-time pilot. I'll split in three or four days."

"Maybe Valentine will be reunited with her family by then," Elli conjectured. "Otherwise, Danner and I will care for her here and handle whatever comes up. If nothing does . . ."

Maybe we can adopt her, West found himself thinking. *Angel would be a great mother and I—* He stopped the sudden, impulsive thought and shifted uncomfortably on the sofa. *What the hell's going on in my brain?*

"I'll call the chief after you finish chewing me out," he muttered.

Elli rose from the sofa. "I've finished for the time being. Phone him and see what's what. Then tell Danner you have travel plans."

WEST WENT to his suite and phoned the chief, who spoke in a whisper and had nothing new to report. West told him to check out Michelle Worth and determine whether she'd had a child six months ago. During the short call, Valentine blithely wet her diaper and one leg of West's pants, as well.

West had to change clothes, wrap Val in a bath towel and take her back to Mallory's suite, where the diapers were. He found Mallory finishing up a phone call to Elli's personal physician, Dr. Ortiz.

"He'll be here in twenty minutes to examine Valentine," she said after hanging up.

West frowned. "Examine her for what?"

"The state of her health, of course. I suggested a general exam to Mrs. C., and she approved. After all, we know nothing about Valentine. The more we learn, the better we'll be able to give her the best care."

West looked down at the baby in his arms. "Who would leave the cutest thing in the world on the back lawn?" He shot a defensive, warning glance at Mallory. "Don't say what you're thinking. She's not my wild oat."

Mallory glanced away. "I wasn't thinking that." Her thoughts were about how much she'd miss him if he went away. And how much she had loved being with him in her bed.

"To prove it," he said, "Ortiz can do blood tests on me and Val. I guarantee they won't match up."

Mallory hoped he was right. Not that a mismatch would negate West's reputation. Nothing could erase that from her mind, especially now that she was part of his past. For a while she'd begun thinking of herself as part of West's future. Now she knew she'd been fooling herself.

"Blood tests are reliable, aren't they?" he asked.

"I wouldn't know."

He scowled. "Neither would I. Nothing like this has ever come up before. And don't say it's a miracle."

"West, you made your own headlines. If you can't take the heat in your own kitchen, get out of it."

Valentine cut them both off by putting up a sudden fuss. West propped her against his shoulder and patted her back to soothe her. She promptly spit up on his sweater.

Mallory had to smile. "Never burp a baby without a cloth over your shoulder."

"I didn't know she'd erupt."

"Wait until she erupts at the other end."

As if taking the hint, Valentine got red faced and made grunting sounds.

West wrinkled his nose. "Pyew. What do I do now?"

Mallory laughed at the expression on his face. "Hold your breath. Let her finish."

"Find me a gas mask, Angel." He started to laugh, too, and pinched his nostrils shut. "Val, you little stinkpot!"

Together they cleaned the baby, rediapered her and sponged the stain out of West's sweater. Mallory made mental notes to put every possible baby supply on Berthe's grocery list.

She also fell just a little bit more in love with West as he manfully dealt with his first really messy cloth diaper—by tossing it in the trash.

A knock sounded on Mallory's door. It was Berthe, accompanied by Edith, Pearl and Rosa.

"Mrs. C. just called us all together about the baby," said Berthe, herding the maids in for a peek. "She swore us to silence."

Like a proud father, West held Valentine up for the housekeeper and maids to see. They ooohed and aaahed, then twittered when West informed them that he could change diapers like a nanny now.

Q and Oddjob showed up and crowded in with the others. Mallory saw them all privately wondering if Valentine had anything personal to do with West.

"As Mrs. C. told you," she reminded them, "everyone's lips are sealed. Saying one word to anyone outside this house will be cause for instant dismissal."

"Oh, Mrs. C. made that clear," Edith assured her.

"*Sí,*" said Rosa. "Everything stays *a puerta cerrada.*" She translated, "Behind closed doors."

The handsome cooks nodded solemnly and Pearl confirmed, "Our lips are zipped."

Berthe piped in, "I'll get everything the supermarket has in the baby section and say it's for one of my grandkids. Powder, lotion, disposable dydies, pacifier."

"The whole enchilada," Rosa quipped with a broad smile.

Mallory was thinking ahead, too. "Don't go to the market until after Dr. Ortiz examines Valentine, Berthe. He might put her on a formula that you'll need to pick up, too."

"What's a formula?" West asked.

Looking as ignorant about formula as West did, the cooks backed out of the room. Berthe and the maids exchanged amused glances.

Mallory replied, "Some babies can't digest mother's milk or cow's milk. They need a prepared formula for nourishment. Dr. Ortiz will know best."

The front doorbell rang.

"That must be him," Bertha said. She herded the maids out and went to answer the door.

A minute later she came back with the doctor to Mallory's suite, then returned to housekeeping. Elli came in and gave him a warm hug.

"Doctor, thank you for coming right away. We have a small problem here, as Danner explained when she called."

"A baby, so it seems," he replied. Genial and smiling, the tall, swarthy, silver-haired physician shook hands with Mallory and West. He then asked for Valentine to be placed on Mallory's bed for the examination.

Elli, Mallory and West gathered around Valentine as the doctor washed his hands in the bathroom. The baby was cooing, kicking her pudgy little feet in the air, sucking on one of her dimpled fists.

"God, she just kills me," West murmured. "I hope nothing's wrong with her."

Dr. Ortiz returned and examined Val. Her heartbeat. Her tiny ears. Her big blue eyes. Her rosebud mouth and pink gums. He measured her and estimated her weight. He pronounced her a healthy, normal, six-month-old child.

"I'll do a blood test, too," he said, "just to make sure."

Everyone around the bed smiled at each other. Then West spoke up. "Can you do a paternity blood test while you're at it, Doctor? For me?"

"If you need one."

"I do," West said firmly. "I know Valentine isn't mine, but only a blood test will prove it."

"Roll up your sleeve," said the doctor, taking the necessary implements out of his medical bag.

He took blood first from West, then from Valentine, who cried bloody murder the moment the brief procedure began. Holding Valentine still for the doctor, Mallory noticed West clenching his fists and grimacing with empathy.

"For pete's sake, don't kill her," he growled at Dr. Ortiz.

"Now, Third, Dr. Ortiz knows what he's doing." Elli took West's arm. "Come into the other room with me."

West resisted. "If anything happens to Val, I—" He broke off, flexing his fists at his sides.

"Dear boy, the way you're bristling, you might as well be her father."

"All finished," said Dr. Ortiz, patting the baby on her head.

West stepped forward and snatched Valentine out of Mallory's hands. "I'll make her feel better."

Valentine quieted immediately, looking up at him from the cradle of his arms. He gave her a loony, spacey grin and crooned, "Dah-dee won't let you get hurt ever again. Okay?"

Dr. Ortiz chuckled. "West, you remind me of Rhett Butler doting on Bonnie Blue in *Gone With the Wind*."

"Exactly," Elli agreed.

Mallory couldn't help falling in love that much more. For the first time, she found herself wishing to have a child of her own—with West. With Valentine she had learned that child care had priceless moments, moments she'd been too young to comprehend with her sisters.

She could appreciate the highs and lows and subtleties of motherhood now, and envision herself giving life, love and care to her own flesh and blood.

West would be a wonderful father. He had been a wonderful lover. He'd be a—

She stopped her thoughts short. He would never be a husband, wonderful or otherwise. She had to keep remembering that and not let it break her heart.

11

TWO DAYS after Dr. Ortiz examined Valentine, the police chief called West with some news. The detective had located records of Michelle Worth having given birth to an illegitimate girl, but Michelle had apparently disappeared or moved out of California. Her family lived in northern Maine. No one knew where she was, or they weren't telling.

Furthermore, Michelle's baby's footprints hadn't been taken at the birth center, since it wasn't the standard procedure. The baby had gone home unnamed. Without prints, there was no way to positively identify Valentine.

"I'll keep on top of it," the chief whispered. "If you spot Ms. Worth anywhere, let me know."

Another call rang in right after that from Dr. Ortiz. "Preliminary tests of your blood and Valentine's exclude you from being her father," the doctor said.

West thanked him, hung up and went to tell Elli and Mallory. Taking with him a little present he'd gotten for Valentine, he found them together with her and the cooks in the kitchen. Q and Oddjob were making baby food.

Valentine was propped on the tile counter in an infant seat, watching Elli and Mallory discuss the menu for a bridge luncheon that Elli would be hosting the next day.

West tied his little gift around Valentine's neck. It was a bib with two words silk-screened on it: SPIT HAPPENS.

They all laughed when they saw it, including Val. He picked her up in the plastic seat and swung her around to make her giggle some more. Everything about her was a constant delight for him.

Learning child care from Mallory was just as much fun, except it hadn't been easy keeping his hands off of his teacher.

Whenever it occurred to him that his feelings for Mallory had gone beyond fun, he played with Val to stop thinking about it. But, then, playing with the baby made him want one of his own. That always circled him back to how he felt about Mallory. Thinking about Mallory, and about getting her pregnant, inevitably got his hormones fired up. He was always trying to calm them down.

It was scary how often he asked himself, *Is this love, this driving desire to possess one woman and have delightful little babes like Valentine with her?*

"I've got some news," he told Elli as Valentine chortled with glee in the dipping, swooping infant seat. ·

"Off to the nursery with us, then," Elli said, motioning Mallory to come and leading the way to Mallory's suite. In privacy there, West told them the test results.

Elli gave him a big hug and further reassurances that she had always believed him. Mallory felt humbled, immensely relieved and more than a little guilty for not giving his word her complete trust.

West went on to report what the chief had said and Mallory listened, feeling heartened that some progress had been made. Yet it was disheartening that Michelle couldn't be located and that Valentine couldn't be ID'd.

Elli said, "Third, what can you remember about Michelle? Any little thing that might help the detective?"

West shrugged. "Nothing personal. She spent her days off somewhere else and never mentioned where. She was so pretty, I figured she had a boyfriend." He shook his head. "What do you recall?"

"Not very much. I was so depressed then, not observant at all. She kept her personal life private—including her love life, apparently. I recall most that she was sweet, honest, even-tempered and very patient with me right up to the day she left." She raised her eyebrows. "Speaking of leaving, are you going away soon, Third?"

He nodded, avoiding Mallory's eyes. "I called an aircraft broker this morning and bought a plane through him. It's based in Honolulu—four-passenger, fully equipped and capable of hopping from island to island around most of the world. He hired me a full-time pilot who's based there, too. I'm set to fly out commercial the day after tomorrow."

Elli clucked her tongue looking at Valentine. "She's going to miss Dah-dee."

"He'll miss her," West said, his eyes uncontrollably meeting up with Mallory's.

Mallory felt a lump forming in her throat. How she would miss West. Teaching him about babies had been so much fun. His curiosity was insatiable. She had begun to see that one baby with two adults caring for it wasn't the burden that mothering triplets had been. It was more of a joyous responsibility with West in the picture.

Soon he would be out of the picture. Day after tomorrow. As her eyes locked with his, her heart almost tore in two.

Elli stood up. "I have to take my afternoon medicine dose." She blew Valentine a kiss and left.

"I'd rather stick around until Val gets reunited with whoever left her here," West said, shoving his hands in his pockets so that he wouldn't reach out for Mallory. "But after the other morning, I guess that's not a good idea."

Mallory murmured, "As far as I'm concerned, you mean."

"Yep." He was silent for a moment, then said, "What are the chances that you'd go out on a date with me after you go to work somewhere else?"

She felt a hopeful smile blossoming on her lips. "What do you think they are?"

"Slim to none. You'd want to go steady, I'll bet."

Her smile eroded. "You wouldn't want to, I'll bet."

"Look, playing the field is my life-style, Angel."

"Play it, then. No one is stopping you."

"I've been too busy with Valentine. Diapers, baby baths—" He waved a hand. "It's always something."

"Valentine isn't your responsibility, West. She's mine, as Mrs. C. has directed."

"You had enough responsibility when you were growing up," he told her. "Take a break and enjoy a helping hand. You haven't thanked me yet for giving you one."

"You've been a big help, West. Thank you, sincerely. And I'm sorry I harbored reservations about you and Michelle."

"It doesn't matter now." He paused, studying her face. "Angel, how long has it been since you spent a day without a care in the world? On most of your days off you do karate practice. Or target practice. Or fly a plane.

"It's part of my job."

"Always on the job, aren't you? Except when you had fun with me. In the fountain. And in bed."

"Please stop reminding me of all the mistakes I've made."

She felt angry with herself that she had made so many missteps—in such a short time. It hurt her that West was ticking off their shared experiences like an accountant adding up some figures. And it hurt that he was right about how much of herself she had put into her job.

"What are you afraid of, Angel? Of letting go and not knowing where you'll end up? Of having the time of your life—with me?"

"What are *you* afraid of, West? Going steady? Making commitments and solid plans? Being faithful?"

"When I'm old and gray," he said.

"If you live that long," she said. And then somber words she didn't expect slipped out. "My mother was your age when she died. Thirty-four."

"When you were twelve," he said, his face and tone softening. "Tell me about it."

She stood and went to the window to look out. The words wouldn't come. She shook her head.

"Some other time, then."

"It wasn't a very bright topic to bring up. I'm sorry. Again. I forgot you lost your mother, too, just last year. It's thoughtless of me to remind you."

"We weren't that close," he said, "but I miss her more than I expected." Joining Mallory at the window, he rubbed her shoulders. "I'm going to miss you, too, when I leave."

"How long will you be gone?"

"Two weeks, maybe three."

She tried to sound flip and casual so he wouldn't know her true feelings. "Back to the playing field."

"For me, it's the only way to go," he said.

Mallory felt his breath stir her hair. She felt his thumbs gently rubbing the tension and loneliness out of her neck and shoulders. She leaned back against him and his arms slipped around her, under her breasts. He immediately started to harden and she could feel his erection rise against the small of her back.

He pulled the curtain shut with one hand. "I can't forget the other morning. I can't stay away from you."

"It does us no good to be intimate, West. I . . . oh . . ."

He began kissing the side of her neck, cupping his hands under the weight of her breasts. "I can't sleep at night," he whispered in her ear. "Can you? *Can* you?"

"Not very well."

"I want you and you want me. What else really matters?"

"My job. My professional reputation." *My heart.* However, her awareness was quickly narrowing to just herself and West, with no other considerations.

He unbuttoned her suit jacket and fanned his finger-tips over her silk blouse, over her nipples. He smoothed one hand down the middle of her skirt, grasped a fist-ful of the material and started inching it upward.

"What about your inner needs, Angel? What about mine?"

Valentine let out a squeal loud enough to turn West's head toward her. He saw her looking, wide-eyed with interest, at him and Mallory. The idea of her observing every erotic move made him hesitate.

"Uh, Val's staring at us, Angel."

"Oh." Mallory eased around in his embrace to look behind him at Val. "Hmm."

"She can't see us if we go in the bedroom."

"West, we can't go that far." Mallory took a shaky step away from him. "We shouldn't even be doing this. What are we getting ourselves into again?"

West sighed. "We can't help it. It's bigger than both of us."

She sank into the armchair because her legs were feeling too boneless to hold her up. "What am I going to do about you?" she asked helplessly.

Off the top of his head West said, "Go on my trip with me. Be my pilot."

"You're crazy, West."

"No, I'm not. A trip together would do us both some good. It—"

The phone rang, cutting him off. Mallory answered. It was Elli, requesting a pot of jasmine tea and a scone.

End of argument, temporarily at least.

THE NEXT MORNING, Oddjob came rushing up to Mallory as she returned from delivering Elli's hot chocolate and newspaper. She had also delivered Valentine, to spend part of the morning with Elli.

"A lady at the back door," he gasped. "Black and blue. Asking for Valentine. I tell her wait. Talk to you."

She hurried to the back door with him. Outside on the step stood a thin, pale young woman with short hair the same red as Val's and blue, bruise-blackened eyes.

Mallory introduced herself. "And you are . . . ?"

"Michelle Worth," she replied in a small, frail voice. It cracked with tears as she added, "I left my baby here. Is she here?"

"Yes, come inside and—"

"Is she okay? Is she?" Great tears welled out of Michelle's battered eyes. She shivered in an oversize quilted coat.

"She's fine. Happy and thriving. Please come inside where it's warm while I ring Mrs. Cade's suite and tell her you've come."

"Just take me to Valentine. Please."

"In just a moment. I know you're anxious." Mallory led her into the kitchen to the house phone. She kept an arm around Michelle's thin, quivering shoulders as she spoke to Elli.

"Bring her to my suite immediately, Danner."

Mallory hung up. "Valentine is with Mrs. Cade up-stairs. Come, I'll take you."

Passing by Oddjob at the six-burner range, Mallory asked him to make hot chocolate and a quick breakfast for Michelle, and to bring the tray upstairs when it was ready.

"Presto," he promised, his dark, handsome eyes round and solemn and riveted on Michelle.

At Elli's door, Mallory knocked. Elli opened it, holding Valentine in her arms.

Michelle's pale, bruised face crumpled. "Oh my God. Oh my God." She reached out for her child, trem-bling, with tears streaming down her hollow cheeks.

Elli's eyes filled, too, first with shock and then with sad recognition. She gave Valentine up into her moth-er's reed-thin arms.

Somehow they all made it to the sofa, where Mi-chelle almost collapsed. Mallory got a box of tissues for the tears that were rolling down every cheek in the room, including Valentine's.

They had all begun to compose themselves when Oddjob came in and presented Michelle with the breakfast he had made especially for her—hot choco-late and miniature, heart-shaped pancakes.

"For beautiful mother and lady," he told her in his melodious old-country accent. He touched his heart and bowed. "From Oddjob."

Michelle was so moved and grateful that she broke down again. Oddjob bowed once more and left, his eyes shining with emotion, too.

It took a while for everything to sort out, but finally things did. Michelle was able to drink the chocolate and eat the pancakes as she kept a tight hold on Valentine. Some color filtered into her pale face as she gained the strength to explain herself.

Hers was a sad, woeful tale of mental and physical abuse by her former boyfriend, Valentine's father; of severe financial difficulties, of fear that the abuse would extend to Valentine.

"I think he—Alex—followed me here," Michelle said. "He tried to steal Valentine away from me so he could control me and make me do anything he wanted. But we got away from him and I didn't know what to do or where to go." Her voice cracked. "I was desperate when I came here that night and heard voices by the fountain."

"It's all right," Elli said soothingly. "We understand. You brought Valentine here where you knew she'd be protected. She's safe here and so are you."

"I don't have a job. I don't have anything, Mrs. Cade. I can't pay you back for what you've done."

Elli patted her hand. "Oh, yes, you can. I remember that you did some excellent sewing work while you were here. I have many clothes from the past that need altering and updating. You'll be my full-time, live-in seamstress, if you want."

"Oh, Mrs. Cade. I'd love to. But the police will put me in jail for abandoning my baby."

"They will not. Third and I won't allow it. We'll vouch for your character ourselves and I'm confident that the chief of police himself will dismiss any and all charges against you." She turned to Mallory. "Is Third up and at 'em yet?"

"I don't know, Mrs. C. Shall I check his suite?"

"Please do. This is news he shouldn't miss. He's got to call off the investigation right away, as only he can."

Mallory crossed the hall to West's suite and knocked. He came to the door with a damp towel fastened around his hips and white shaving foam frosting his face.

"Angel. What a surprise!"

She stepped inside the door and closed it, then began telling him what had happened. He motioned her into the bathroom with him, where he continued shaving and she continued explaining.

They both finished at the same time and stood looking at each other in the mirror.

"Great," he said brightly. "Val gets to stay home with Dah-dee." His face clouded. "Except he'll be leaving home tomorrow." He brightened again. "He'd better postpone his trip until everything gets settled around here."

"It's probably a good idea," Mallory agreed, "since you're the one blackmailing the chief. Also, Alex sounds like a tough customer who might cause trouble."

West nodded. "Sounds like it to me, too."

"He might think twice about getting tough if you're around, West."

West flexed his biceps. "I'll break him in two if he touches Valentine Worth." He sobered. "Michelle's in pretty bad shape, huh?"

"Shocking shape. She apparently loved Alex. Maybe still does. I think she'll need a lot of counseling."

He shook his head. "It's a shame. She's a beautiful lady who deserves better. What's Alex's last name?"

"Riggs."

The phone in West's bathroom rang. He picked it up and had a brief, monosyllabic conversation before hanging up.

"Looks like I'm leaving home, whether I want to or not," he said. "One of my old sailing buddies wants to buy an island right now. Tiare Island. Rotten timing, though."

Mallory said, "I can start wearing my gun if Alex makes it necessary."

West rinsed his face, then gave her a long look in the mirror. "I don't want you in danger."

"West, security is part of my job if it's called for."

"You weren't on the job when you put yourself on the line to save Aunt. You could have gotten killed."

"I wouldn't have gotten this job otherwise."

"Now you're looking for another one."

She shrugged and repeated, "Security is part of my job."

"I prefer another solution. I'll hire someone from outside to watch the house," West said. "Why don't you do something for yourself for a change? Forget taking care of everyone and come with me on my sales trip, Angel." He toweled the rinse water from his face. "See what happens when you don't have anybody to take care of but you."

"I know what will happen, West."

"Me, too," he said, looking into the mirror at her. "We'll make love night and day. It's inevitable."

Mallory drew a deep breath, unable to tear her eyes from his reflection in the mirror. His potent, masculine reflection.

"West—" she licked her lips "—what's happening between us?"

He turned around and gave her an honestly baffled look. "Don't ask me. I only know what to do about it." He pulled her into his arms. "Why don't we just do what we can?"

Mallory flattened her palms on his bare chest. "You don't love me, West. You just want . . . sex."

"That's not all I want, Angel. Not with you. With you it's different. Or are you saying it's not different for you with me?"

"No. It's special for me, too. But if I decide to go on your trip with you—"

"You will?"

"I'm thinking about it. You're making it hard not to."

"Good." He grinned.

"West, I'll think about going away with you." It would be her first and last fling, she reasoned. All the fun she'd never had. When it came to an end, she'd be a good sport.

"You don't have much time to mull it over."

"Before time runs out, I'll make the right decision."

He reluctantly let go of her. "We both want each other. Just make sure you decide in our mutual favor."

12

EARLY THE NEXT MORNING, when Mallory was serving Elli hot chocolate and a newspaper, West came into his aunt's suite.

"Our philandering police chief says Valentine's case is closed. Nothing left on the record."

Elli clapped her hands. "I knew it all along."

Mallory smiled. "Michelle will be relieved."

Elli's telephone rang and Mallory stopped serving to answer it. "Mrs. Cade's quarters. May I help you?"

"Yeah," said a cool, smooth male voice. "You've got something of mine in your big, bad house and I know it."

"Who is speaking, please?"

The voice snickered. "Wouldn't you like to know, you old bat. Don't try to stand between me and what's mine."

"Please identify yourself, sir," Mallory commanded.

"Keep me away from my property and see what happens. You'll see, you dried-up old hag." The line went dead.

"Who is it, Danner?"

Troubled, Mallory replaced the receiver. "He wouldn't reveal his name, but I suspect it was Alex

Riggs making threats." She repeated to West and Elli what the caller had said.

"How rude," said Elli, looking distressed.

West was scornful. "He thinks they're his property?"

"His meaning seems pretty clear," Mallory said. "If he knows they're here, it could mean trouble."

"Michelle said she was afraid that Alex had followed her here yesterday," Elli recalled. "She said he was a manager of some sort for the telephone company before getting fired recently. That must be how he got my private, unlisted number."

Mallory nodded. "He sounded determined as well as rude."

"Maybe he's just bluffing, scratching around for a clue to where Val and Michelle are," West said. "Luckily, you didn't tip him off one way or the other, Angel."

Elli fretted. "I don't want him anywhere near here. It breaks my heart to see what he did to her."

Mallory raised her eyebrows at West. "Maybe the call should be reported to the police."

"Knowing them, they'll laugh it off as a routine prank call," West said. "We don't have any proof that it was Alex." He paused, then decided, "If he calls again, we'll report it. It could just be a bluff, as I said."

"In case it's not, I'll start carrying my gun on duty," Mallory said.

"Yes, Danner. Better to be safe than sorry if he comes around here."

West said, "To make sure he doesn't, I'll hire a couple of private eyes to shadow him. I'll find out from

Michelle where he lives and then make some calls. I want ex-cops, if possible, who can start today."

"Dear Third." Elli sighed, watching him leave to make the calls from his own phone. "Danner, I feel better already with you and Third both helping out."

"Mrs. C., I'd better have the numbers changed for every phone line in the house. I'll also read the phone company the riot act for letting your unlisted number out."

"It might get out again if that Alex is clever enough," Elli cautioned, "but go ahead and make changes right away. Also, tell Michelle that she and Valentine shouldn't leave the house for any reason."

"I'll be sure to."

"And please tell Third to postpone his trip."

"No need, Mrs. C. He mentioned yesterday that he'd put off leaving for a few days. I'll take care of everything else right now."

AFTER TALKING to the phone company and alerting Michelle, Mallory went to her own suite. She loaded her revolver and put it into its shoulder holster. Wearing it in place under her suit jacket, she opened her door to return to her duties and found Edith poised to knock on it.

The maid was breathless. "I was washing windows in the library and saw a man climb the fence into the backyard."

"When?"

"Just now. He looked young and well dressed."

"Edith, where are Michelle and Valentine?"

"In the south-wing sewing room. She's raising hems."

"Go there and stay with her until I come back. Lock the sewing-room door from inside—and take Rosa or Pearl with you if you see them along your way. Hurry."

"Yes, Miss Danner." Edith rushed to the south wing.

Mallory sped to the kitchen. "Q, Oddjob, come with me. We have an intruder in the backyard."

The cooks abandoned their tasks and followed her to the back door. She opened it and found a good-looking, dark-haired young man reaching for the outside knob. He covered his surprise with a smart-aleck smirk.

"Yo, babe," he said, his eyes lazily measuring her bustline. His expression grew wary when the cooks stepped up behind her.

Mallory asked, "Are you expected here, sir?"

"Yeah, I'm expected here. An appointment with a maid."

"Would that be Pearl, Edith or Rosa?"

His ice-blue eyes narrowed in his handsome face. "Not them. The personal maid," he answered cockily.

"There are no other maids employed here. You must be at the wrong address."

"Who are you?" he inquired, eyeing her speculatively.

"The butler."

Knowing he must be Alex Riggs—whom Michelle had said resembled John Travolta—Mallory surmised that he didn't know things had changed at the mansion. She decided to make one thing perfectly clear to him. So that he could clearly see her holster and weapon, she unbuttoned her suit jacket and slipped it off.

Alex took a step back, and so did the cooks. Mallory could hear them draw in a startled breath. Then she heard West behind her saying tersely, "What's going on back here?"

"We have an unexpected visitor, Mr. Cade." She put her jacket on as West joined her at her side. "I was just telling him he must be at the wrong address."

Alex's icy eyes narrowed again and he backed away another step. "Yeah. It's starting to look like it. Well, nice talking to you."

"We'll all show you to the rear gate," Mallory told him. She pointed behind him. "That way."

Alex turned Gucci loafers in the opposite direction and sauntered to the gate as if he were totally innocent of any ulterior motive. He even whistled a catchy tune on the way, cocking his hands in the pockets of his stylish, pleated trousers as though he were taking a stroll in the sunshine.

"Classy spread," he commented lightly, gazing out over the fountain, the gazebo, the tennis court.

"No trespassing allowed at any time," West informed him, his tone as frigid as Alex's eyes.

Alex shrugged it off. "My mistake, man. Just got the wrong address and the wrong back door, that's all."

Mallory unlocked the rear gate and held it open for him. "Be sure not to get it wrong again," she warned as he passed through into the back alley.

"Oh, I'll be extra sure to get it right the next time," Alex assured her.

He got into a Mustang convertible parked in the alley and drove away. Mallory made a mental note of the car's navy blue color and the license-plate number.

"Good riddance, jerk," West said and rebolted the lock on the thick, wooden gate.

"Bad dude," Q muttered in a thick Hungarian accent.

"Michelle's bad dude, I bet," Oddjob growled.

Mallory confirmed that he was right and cautioned, "We all have to keep an eye out for him. He might sneak back when he thinks no one is looking."

She knew that one of the cooks would be especially vigilant, for a personal reason. Oddjob had fallen for Michelle. With him around, Michelle would be that much safer. At least, Mallory hoped so.

THE NEXT DAY Mallory received a letter from London. Lady Eaton wrote that Lord Eaton's butler had won a derby sweepstakes and quit the job. She was offering Mallory the position if she was interested.

Mallory's first thought was that London was half a world away from San Francisco—and from West. Loving him, and feeling devoted to Ellinor, she was torn. Rationally she knew a move to London would remove her from her problem. There, in time, she could hope to forget West Cade. She could be a proper, upright, faultless butler again.

Lady Eaton had written:

Take your time deciding. It would be a big move for you, and you'd want to give Mrs. Cade reasonable notice. But don't take too long, Danner. The house here can't go for more than a month without a strong manager. You, I hope.

Relieved that she didn't have to make a sudden decision, Mallory kept the job offer to herself and concentrated on her current responsibilities. It was a big help that West had hired two private eyes to watch Alex Riggs day and night. They had started yesterday afternoon, not long after Alex had trespassed onto the property.

It took the pressure off, but Mallory kept her gun under her jacket as a precaution. Everyone in the house was security-conscious now, careful not to reveal Michelle's presence to anyone on the outside. Michelle was settling into her seamstress role and Dr. Ortiz had come this morning to examine her bruises. Valentine continued being everyone's little sweetheart—especially West's.

Late that same afternoon the private eyes called from Las Vegas. Alex had driven there overnight, apparently to gamble. They were on his trail, keeping a close watch.

Everyone in the house breathed a sigh of relief after they heard that bit of good news from West. So when he called Mallory to his suite later that evening saying he wanted to discuss something with her, she was in good spirits.

She entered and found him mixing two *mai tais* at his bar. Hawaiian music played in the background. "Lovely Hula Hands" was the melodious tune.

"*Two* drinks?" she questioned. "You know I never drink on the job."

"Tonight you do." He motioned her to take a seat on his rattan sofa and handed her a crystal glass. "Aunt gives you her permission through me. Honest." He gave a Boy Scout salute.

Mallory accepted the *mai tai* and returned his smile. He was so . . . infectious. And he was making it that much harder to turn down his offer to join him on his trip.

West settled next to her and propped his feet up on the teak coffee table. He clinked his glass against hers and proposed a toast.

"To our upcoming trip."

"Not so fast, West. I haven't made any decisions."

"Well, I've gotten you Aunt's permission to fly to Honolulu with me and be my pilot from there to the island I'm going to sell. She says it's fine with her if it's fine with you."

"You said you hired your own pilot, West." She was stalling for time, still unsure what to do.

"I decided I'd rather have you at the controls for this trip, Angel. You said you might go. I'm helping you decide."

Mallory sipped her drink. It was sweet, tart and delicious. She tried to think rationally and line up all the reasons she shouldn't go with West.

She said, "The whole household will know we're together. They won't be thinking it's just business."

"I knew you'd say that, Angel. So I've figured it all out. My plan is that I'll leave here to start my sales trip, and you'll leave here the day after I do. Aunt Elli's going to tell everyone the little white lie that you have a family emergency in Tucson. No one will be the wiser. Berthe will be temporarily in charge for you."

"What if Dad happens to call here from Tucson for me. What then?"

West shrugged. "Phone him and chat the day before you leave. You usually call him rather than him calling you, anyway, right?"

"West, Michelle and Valentine need armed protection. If I leave—"

He held up a hand. "With two PI's on Alex's heels, Michelle and Val have nothing to fear. And there are already two strong, intimidating men in the house—Q and Oddjob."

"How would I explain a tropical tan when I return?"

"Tucson gets a lot of sun."

"I don't have clothes for islands."

"No problem for a filthy-rich guy. I'll take you on a shopping spree in Honolulu the first day."

"You're famous as well as rich," she pointed out. "We might get photographed together by the *National Enquirer*, or something."

He shook his head. "I know how to avoid the *paparazzi* when I want to." Sliding one arm behind her on the back of the sofa, he murmured, "Come on an adventure with me, Angel—without a care in the world."

She raised her eyes and looked into his. He made it sound like a dream. Fabulous fun and nothing to worry about.

"What if something goes wrong?"

"What if it doesn't? Come on. Let yourself loose for a change." He leaned forward and placed a soft, coaxing kiss on her lips. "Say yes."

"Yes." She couldn't stop the word from slithering out. The devil, the *mai tai* and the hula music were making her do it. To keep them from making her do more than have a drink on the job, she stood up and set her glass down. "Let me know when to leave."

"My flight leaves at 8:15 tomorrow morning," he said. "You fly out the next day at the same time. Your ticket will be at the airport, waiting for you. Take a cab. I'll meet your flight in Honolulu." He came to his feet beside her. "No second thoughts, okay?"

"Okay." She knew she'd have at least a few, but she wouldn't let them stop her. She eluded another kiss from West and went to the door, knowing she'd hula with him all night if she didn't leave at once.

"Good night, West."

He grinned and winked at her. "Aloha, Angel."

THE NEXT MORNING, Mallory was nervous, on edge, having lots of second thoughts. Yet deep inside she was burning with anticipation and excitement.

She began her day by saving Ellinor a little white lie. After explaining to the staff that there was a family emergency in Tucson, she took Elli's morning tray upstairs.

"Good morning, Mrs. C."

Elli was sitting up in a bed full of cats, looking supremely content and happy. "Danner," she said, "I've been pondering life and cats. I can't imagine a day without four felines anymore." She paused. "And I'm not sure how we'll all get along without you for the next few days."

"I'm not sure I should be going with West, Mrs. C."

"He told me you said yes last night."

Mallory nodded as she poured Elli's hot chocolate. "I did, but now . . ."

"Danner, life is full of risks. Some you should avoid. Some you shouldn't. This is one you shouldn't. I'm glad to tell a white lie to the staff for your reputation's sake."

"I already told the lie myself, Mrs. C."

"Good for you. Nothing else needs to be said about it, then. When you return, you can decide what you'll do with the rest of your life."

"Before I go," Mallory said, "I want you to know that Lady Eaton wrote to me. Lord Eaton's butler quit and I'm being offered the position."

After a moment of silent surprise, Elli said, "You'll have the time you need to weigh your options in the tropics. And Third will have time to weigh his."

"I'm afraid it's a mistake to go away with him."

"So what if it is?" Elli waved a hand. "Only the three of us will ever know. Now, please tell Michelle I'll see her in thirty minutes for a fitting."

"Thirty minutes," Mallory confirmed.

Elli took up her hot chocolate and inhaled the aroma. "Have a safe trip, Danner. I'll be thinking of you and Third—and hoping for the best."

Mallory went to Michelle's room and knocked. As Mallory had cautioned her for security reasons, Michelle didn't unlock or open her door. She came to it and asked first, "Who is it?"

"Danner. Good morning."

Michelle opened the door. "Hi. Come in. I'm in the middle of changing Valentine's diaper, so hold your nose."

Mallory smiled and followed her to Valentine. "How are you coming along so far, Michelle?"

"Great. I feel so much better...and safer. I even slept all night last night."

Mallory told her about her impending departure to Tucson and about West's trip to Hawaii. She reiterated that Michelle should feel safe and secure now that the private investigators were monitoring Alex twenty-four hours a day.

"How will I ever pay Mr. Third and Mrs. Cade back for all they've done, Miss Danner?" Michelle frowned as she diapered the baby. "I mean, I know they're super rich and all, but . . ."

"Don't worry about that. They're generous people and love sharing their bounty. They both enjoy Valentine more than they can say. We all do."

Michelle smiled. "You always know just the right thing to say. This house is so different now that Mrs. Cade isn't depressed anymore. She told me you've made the big difference and hired all the right help for her."

"That's what butlers are for, Michelle."

Michelle smoothed the silky red hair on her baby's head with a loving hand. She mused, "Isn't it weird that Valentine doesn't look anything like Alex? Even her eyes aren't the same blue as his. Not a mean, freeze-out blue." Her mouth tightened. "I can't believe I ever loved him."

"Love can be unreasonable," Mallory said, thinking of her unreasonable love for West.

"He kept stringing me along, promising he'd marry me. Now I know he just kept me around to beat up on.

After he'd slug me, he'd cry and say he was sorry and he'd never do it again. He'd be so sweet and nice, you can't imagine."

Mallory saw Michelle's bruised eyes fill with tears. She soothed, "He's not worth crying over. Your eyes can't take any more tears, either."

Michelle dabbed them gingerly with a tissue. "I got so trapped in his power trip, Miss Danner. I couldn't break out of it for so long. I never thought anything this awful would ever happen to me."

"It's not going to happen again, Michelle. That's the good news. You have a fresh start and everyone here is on your side."

"There you go again, saying all the right things." Michelle ducked her head shyly.

"I mean every word. And if you haven't happened to notice, Oddjob is especially on your side."

Michelle blushed, looking pleased. "He sent me flowers yesterday." She pointed at a mixed bouquet on her windowsill. "Aren't they pretty?"

"Yes, it was very thoughtful of him." Mallory had to clear a catch of emotion from her own throat. "I came to say that Mrs. C. will be ready for her fitting in twenty minutes."

"I'll be there." Michelle smiled brightly. "With bells on."

13

THE TEMPERATURE was a balmy eighty-five degrees when Mallory's flight landed at Honolulu International Airport.

After disembarking from the 747, she didn't see West in the crowd waiting to greet the arriving passengers. She hesitated outside of the exit gate, clutching her carry-on suitcase, looking around for him. A touch on her elbow startled her.

"Miss Mallory Danner?" inquired a trim, slim, middle-aged Japanese man. He wore a tailored black suit and carried a lush, ginger-orchid lei draped over one arm.

"Yes, I'm Danner."

"Aloha." He placed the lei around her neck. "Mr. Cade waits in his limousine outside. I'm Yoshitaka Hashimoto, his chauffeur. Call me 'Yoshi.' I'll carry your bag, please."

"Aloha, Yoshi. Thank you." She gave the carryon to him. "This is the sum total of my luggage."

He guided her through the crowded terminal, explaining, "It's elbow to elbow here during the peak travel periods. Mr. Cade was wary of being recognized."

Outside at the curb, Yoshi opened the door to a Mercedes-Benz limousine. Mallory found West seated inside, pouring Dom Perignon into a crystal champagne flute.

"Aloha, Angel. Step right in and sit next to me."

She did and Yoshi shut the door behind her. There was no turning back now, she thought. "Aloha, West."

He handed her the bubbling glass and poured another for himself from the built-in bar. The partition between the driver and passenger sections of the limousine was shut. The windows had a one-way tint, allowing passengers to look out but no one outside to look in. She was alone, in luxurious privacy, with the hottest date in the world.

"Smooth flight?" he inquired.

"It couldn't be otherwise in the VIP deluxe cabin. Thank you." She touched her orchid lei. "Thank you for this, too."

"Only the best of the best for my top-flight personal pilot, Angel." He toasted, "To a high-flying getaway."

The limo started up and pulled away, but the ride was so smooth she could hardly feel it. There was tropical heat outside, but the air in the limo was cool and conditioned, spiced by the scent of fine leather and the fragrance of her lei.

West was dressed in pleat-front white trousers and an open-collared white shirt that conveyed the impression of a modern-day pirate. Mallory felt overdressed in the skirt of her lightest weight wool suit with a silk blouse and low heels. The exotic orchids helped her feel less ill suited.

West took her hand in his. "How are things back home?"

"Berthe is in temporary charge of the staff. Everyone but Mrs. C. thinks I'm in Tucson because of a family illness."

"Good," West said. "Every day from now on is Fun Day."

Mallory gave him a sidelong look and teased, "There must be some work involved in selling an island."

"Not the way I sell islands, Angel. You'll see."

She glanced out the window. "Where are we going?"

"To a hotel that knocks itself out to give its guests pure luxury and total privacy. The Kahala. I've booked a suite for tonight. Three bedrooms."

"Three?"

"Why not? One for you. One for me." He grinned, a perfect devil. "And one for lots of F-U-N!"

MALLORY WAS FEELING quite bubbly by the time the limo arrived at the Kahala. In the ocean-view suite, West showed her the bedroom he'd chosen for her. He'd had it filled with fragrant tropical blossoms that made it a bower of flowers. A wicker basket overflowed with ripe papayas and mangoes.

To her astonishment, her closet was hung with all the clothes she could possibly wish to wear in the tropics, from silk evening sarongs to Bermuda shorts and bikinis. Her dresser drawers contained neat, silky piles of lingerie and fine hosiery. Her shoe rack held tennies, espadrilles, sandals and evening slippers. Everything was her size.

Mallory was overwhelmed. "West, what have you done?"

"Don't thank me," he said. "Your total surprise is thanks enough. You like everything so far?"

Mallory gazed around in wonder. "It's too much."

"Not really." He shrugged. "Whatever you don't use can be returned if you insist. Come and see my room."

It was also just as lavish, with lots of flowers and island fruit. His bed, like hers, was king-size and banked with a double tier of downy pillows.

"And the 'f-u-n' room is where?" she asked with a wry smile.

He laughed. "Nowhere. I said that to make your cheeks pink. Just playing around. Why don't you change into something cool and comfortable? I'll order lunch to be served on our lanai."

Mallory changed clothes, feeling dazed. She had a tough time deciding between a Hawaiian print halter dress and a silky shorts-and-shirt outfit. The clothes were a perfect fit, including a pair of thong sandals. She chose the dress, feeling daring without a bra or nylons.

West gave her a soft wolf whistle when she joined him on the ocean-view lanai. The latticed arbor brimmed over with fragrant white bougainvillea. Doves cooed and sparrows chirped among the lush leaves. Mallory sank into the rattan patio chair the room service waiter held out for her.

She sighed with tremulous pleasure and gazed out at the South Pacific. *Paradise*.

The waiter served lunch with grace and style, then disappeared. They had grilled mahi-mahi with macadamia coulis, Maui onion bread, and a floral fruit salad. There was iced red hibiscus tea and mango mousse for dessert. As they ate with relish, their conversation was leisurely, inconsequential.

West shared what he knew about the Kahala and its illustrious history. "I'm told that Queen Elizabeth spent a couple of nights here. King Juan Carlos and Queen Sophia of Spain spent part of their honeymoon. And now it's especially notable because we're here, Angel."

She sipped her scarlet tea and tried not to think of how many women he must have brought to this suite.

"This is the first time I've stayed at the Kahala," he added, as if intuiting her thoughts. "Truly."

West found himself thinking that he'd make a habit of staying there with Mallory. He'd come back with her soon to stay longer than one night. They'd return every year together and make it a ritual—a family tradition.

Every year? Family? Stunned by his wayward thoughts, West pushed them out of his mind. He should be thinking about fun, spelled S-E-X.

Yet, as he looked at Mallory, he wondered if she felt up to letting the good times roll. She might be suffering jet lag. She might need a nap. She worked so hard at home and was always up before everyone else every morning. She was probably stifling a polite, weary yawn behind her dreamy smile.

He forced himself to say, "I have some phone calls to make while you get some rest this afternoon. You'll need it for flying tomorrow."

She shook her head slightly. "I'm not really very tir—"

"Sure, you are," he cut in, rising from his chair, assisting her out of hers. "You're just trying to be polite about it. I can tell. I know you better than you think.

Anyway, I've got business to do on the phone, so it's just as well."

He solicitously herded her to the doorway of her room, where he placed a tiny kiss on her forehead and shooed her inside. He shut the door, murmuring, "Sleep well."

Mallory gave the closed door a disbelieving blink. She'd been expecting West to suggest a nap after lunch, but not a real one. It surprised her how tender and loving he'd been, so visibly concerned for her well-being. It seemed as if he really cared—that having fun right away wasn't as important to him as she was.

How sweet. He'd acted courtly, almost old-fashioned, as if afraid that she'd faint from fatigue. How ironic that she felt anything but tired.

Perplexed yet charmed, she undressed and took a cool shower to dampen her sexiest spirits. Wearing one of the six silk nightshirts he'd bought for her, she stretched out on her big bed among the pillows and marveled about West.

What a total surprise.

WEST WAITED in agony for Mallory to rest up. He made several unnecessary phone calls, paced the floor, took a frigid shower and changed into Bermuda shorts. He stared at MTV, made more unnecessary calls and sat for several minutes listening to the phone company's time recording. Every second was torture.

He could have gone snorkeling or beachcombing, but he didn't want her to wake and find him gone. He wanted to be ready and waiting for her. He wanted to take her to another kind of paradise.

Later he'd whisk her away to dinner at a secluded beachfront restaurant where he had reserved a private dining lanai for two. He'd never dined there with anyone before and wasn't sure why exclusivity seemed important now.

Probably because she was different, he decided. After all, she was the first female butler he'd ever known. That alone made her unique.

He clicked off the TV in his room and growled in frustration through clenched teeth. The phone on his bed stand rang, a diversion at last. He picked it up.

"West," a soft, whispery voice said. "It's Mallory. Are you through making your calls?"

Angel! "Through," he confirmed. "All through." He gulped, feeling dizzy with anticipation.

She half whispered, "I'm awake."

"You are?" He almost went through the roof.

"I'm also thirsty," she said. "Is there some champagne left?"

"Lots of it!" he exclaimed, losing his head. "I'll get it. I'll bring it. You just stay right there. In bed. Your bed."

West couldn't believe how he was babbling, but it was beyond him to recapture his earlier aplomb. One hour of agony had pushed him past being cool.

"Don't move, Angel. I'm coming. In a flash."

He bungled the receiver onto its cradle, stuffed his pockets with condoms, then sped through the suite to the wet bar. He bobbled a bottle of Moét out of the minifridge and grabbed two glasses. Water glasses, but what did that matter at a time like this? He raced to Mallory's room and burst through the door.

His temperature went sky-high when he saw her lying on the bed in the hot-pink silk nightshirt he'd bought her. It rode high on her sleek thighs and several of the pearly buttons were undone down the front. Best of all, she was giving him the most playful smile.

He gulped again and felt his eyes bug out. "I thought you'd never wake up."

"I thought you'd never finish your calls," she murmured, undoing one of the pearl buttons. "Every time I dialed, your line was busy."

She undid another button and he dropped the bottle. It hit the thick carpet and rolled somewhere. The glasses went tumbling after it.

"Angel. My God." He took a step forward, feeling almost dumbstruck. "You're so beautiful. So . . . luscious."

Mallory was thrilled to hear him say that. She *felt* luscious. And hot, sexy and pent-up after a whole hour of waiting for him. Something had come over her. She wasn't her old serious self. She was someone new and exciting.

"I'm all rested up, West." She held her arms out to him invitingly. "And I've missed you so much."

West almost killed himself stripping off his clothes. Hands full of condoms he dove onto the bed and landed with a thud. He rained eager kisses all over Mallory's face and lips, while fumbling to undo the rest of her buttons.

"Angel," he panted, tugging at the pearls without success, "you make me crazy. And clumsy. How do I get you out of this thing?"

"I have five more just like it. Just rip it in two."

West grasped the silk in one hand and tore it right off her body. Her skin flushed with heat as he caressed her breasts, then suckled the pink tips. He moved from one to the other, again and again with feverish ardor.

Mallory boldly led his hand between her legs, urging him to feel how ready she was to make love with him. Just as boldly, she curled her hands around his throbbing shaft and West groaned in response.

They rolled over the bed together in the grip of passion, scattering pillows everywhere. Mallory emerged above West, straddling his hips. Using her position of power to full advantage, she played her fingers over his nipples and watched him grimace with pleasure. Circling her tongue around each one, she gloried in the strangled sounds he made. Swaying above him, she felt bold and passionate as she ripped a foil packet open between her teeth.

She sheathed him and sank down on him, filled her body with his strength. As he moved under her, she moved upon him. Her gasps and sighs and moans intermingled with his, rising higher, higher. Then he touched the tip of his finger to where she was joined with him and her pleasure intensified tenfold. He gazed straight into her eyes as her breath caught and held.

I love you, she thought at the last, trembling moment.

"West!" Bursting sensation hurled her to breathless, mindless, timeless rapture.

"Angel!" West arched up into her clasping, pulsing heat.

Together as one, they were lost in paradise.

THE NEXT DAY, Mallory studied a flight map and consulted with a pilot who had flown small planes among the Polynesian islands for twenty-five years. She then filed a detailed flight plan and took the controls of West's new twin-engine plane. The hangar crew had checked it out—and given it a clean bill of health.

Thanks to Yoshi, all the luggage they needed was packed in the cargo hold. He promised he'd be there to meet them on the day they planned to return.

Finally Mallory warmed up the twin engines, West fastened his seat belt and away they flew to the private island of Tiare.

It was an easy course, two hours' time from Oahu to tiny Tiare, which had its own well-maintained landing strip.

"What a day," West said when they reached cruising altitude in sunny skies.

Mallory raised an eyebrow at him. "What a night."

"We'll have more just like it on Tiare," he promised.

He had already told her about the impressive house on the island, and the whirlpool hot tub in the master suite. They'd have the island and the house all to themselves until his client, Andy Pitcairn, arrived by yacht tomorrow morning. Except for the caretaker, who lived a mile away, they'd be alone with each other.

Mallory almost did a hula in the pilot's seat just thinking about it. She was living for the moment, as she had never done in her life, and flying higher than the mere wings of the plane could carry her. It didn't matter right now that her heart would soon be broken. Having the time of her life with West was all that mattered. Right now.

"You're glowing, Angel."

"As if you don't know why."

They laughed together and teased each other mercilessly all the way to Tiare. Two hours later, they landed on the private airstrip. West had radioed ahead to the caretaker, Yoshi's cousin, to meet the plane and drive them to the house.

Mallory discovered that Kenji was much younger than Yoshi, and was an intense young novelist who was writing his first book. Caretaking an Irish rock-star's island getaway gave him the time and solitude to write. He dropped them at the house with their luggage and drove away.

As he had advised, the kitchen was stocked with food and wine. Solar photovoltaic and diesel generators provided power and there was fresh, running water from a natural aquifer. It was an escapist's dream.

Just for fun, West swept Mallory up in his arms and carried her over the threshold of the teak-furnished master suite. He kissed her mercilessly and then tossed her straight into the whirlpool hot tub.

Later that day, Mallory sunbathed nude after skinny-dipping with West in Tiare's blue lagoon. It was a day of firsts.

"GLAD YOU'RE HERE, Angel?"

"This is bliss," Mallory replied as they breakfasted on the stone terrace the next morning. The warm island trade winds played caressingly on her bare skin. She had never felt so relaxed and carefree, so unlike a butler.

West laughed. "Watch out or you'll get hooked on island living the way Captain Cook did. Cook even coined a word for it. Imparadised." He settled back in his patio chair and savored his Kona coffee. "You were born to wear that bikini, you know."

"I don't know why I bothered," she said, waving a hand at his nude body. "I'll only get tan lines out of it."

"I'd like to get *you* out of it, Angel." He stood up from the table to act on his provocative wish, but the crackling sound of the shortwave radio in the house stopped him. He went in to see who was making contact.

Gazing across the terrace to the coral sand beach and the ocean beyond, Mallory glimpsed a whale spout. Yesterday, snorkeling in the lagoon's undersea garden, she had seen tropical sea life of every shape and brilliant color. Breathtaking.

As she finished her share of the ripe, juicy papaya that West had picked from a tree for breakfast, he came out of the house wearing a wide grin. "Andy's running late in his yacht," he said. "Two days off schedule."

"That must be good news," she surmised from his smile.

West's grin widened. "What shall we do with all our extra time alone, now that Andy Pitcairn will be late?"

"Hmm." She pretended to think "What *haven't* we done?".

He leaned down and whispered in her ear.

By the afternoon, Mallory had learned how to make love with him on a floating surfboard in the lagoon. They forgot to use protection that one time, but only worried about it for a minute or two. Worrying in paradise was impossible.

Their next two days together were variations on one theme—intimate togetherness. She learned from him how to live in the moment, how to enjoy for enjoyment's sake. Free of duty and obligation for the first time since her childhood, she abandoned herself to exuberant pleasure.

Being in love didn't alarm her as it had in the city. On the island it seemed only natural to love her constant playmate. She thought West might be in love, too, though he never said so. He acted like a devoted lover, though, always hungry for her and lovingly considerate.

"I may never get enough of you, Angel," he murmured the second morning after the yacht had radioed.

She hoped it would hold true, but she didn't say so.

Later, after more lovemaking and a long noontime nap, she left him sleeping and wandered inland to gather fruit and flowers. Bare-breasted with a *pareu* fastened low on her hips, she returned with a basket full of Tiare's bounty.

West came out to meet her. "Andy radioed while you were gone," he told her. "He's due to arrive midafternoon."

Mallory set down the basket and gave him a devilish smile. "That leaves us just a few more hours alone together. And I know just what we're going to do with them."

14

THE YACHT ARRIVED and dropped anchor in Tiare Bay. West and Mallory motored a dinghy out to greet Andy Pitcairn and his crew.

Approaching the sleek cruiser, Mallory was taken aback to see four bikini-clad women waving to her and West from the deck. Statuesque and gorgeous, they stood two on either side of a darkly tanned, handsome man of about West's age.

She also noticed that the yacht was named *The Party Animal* and she remembered West's saying that the yachtsman was an old sailing buddy of his. It began to seem likely that he and West had often sailed the seas together with this party-girl crew—or one like it.

She gave West a high eyebrow. "You didn't mention the centerfolds."

"I didn't know about them," West muttered. "Andy said he had a surprise on board, but—" He broke off, shrugging.

"A female surprise," Mallory said, disliking the strangers in paradise on sight. "He seems to be the only male on board."

West muttered, "He might be."

Mallory got the whole picture at a glance. She saw that Andrew Pitcairn was a good-time buddy of West's. He had arrived expecting West to revel in playboy heaven with him. West had already confirmed that they'd sailed together in the past, which meant that they might have reveled before on this same island. With four women—or more. Her heart sank.

"Party, party, party," Andy said as he heartily clapped West on the back.

"Yeah." West returned the backslap. "Right."

Yeah? Right? Mallory began grinding her teeth. She paused only to give Andy a fake smile when West introduced her. "Nice to meet you," she lied, shaking Andy's hand.

"The more the merrier," Andy said, turning to introduce his companions. "Eden, Crystal, Sable, Farrah."

Mallory refrained from rolling her eyes at their unlikely names. She observed that West was acknowledging Andy's introduction with a seemingly unforced smile.

The four ladies weren't forcing theirs, either, she noted. They were flashing their pearly whites to the best of their ability at the world's hottest date.

"Andy," said Crystal with a tiny, reproving pout, "West remembers us from the last time. Two years ago, in the Bahamas." She gleamed a smile at West. "Don't you?"

West cleared his throat. "Sure."

Mallory had an intense desire to get off the yacht that minute—*after* pushing West overboard.

"So, Andy," West said. "Tiare's what you think you're looking for, eh?"

Andy replied, "If it's everything you've talked it up to be, I'll even buy it. So far, so good."

"Come ashore and look at the house," West invited.

"Tomorrow," said Andy. "It's party time right now. Mallory, what about a drink? You name it, we've got it."

"Just seltzer with a slice of lime, please."

"That's all?" he said, looking mystified.

West spoke up, "Mallory's my pilot. She's got to stay in A-1 shape to show you aerial views of Tiare tomorrow."

Mallory hoped he might add that she was also his exclusive companion, but he didn't. He ordered a *mai tai* and motioned for her to sit in the canvas chair Andy was pulling out for her at a big deck table. She sat and everyone else took a chair, except for Farrah, who was mixing the drinks at the deck-side bar.

West continued a leisurely sales pitch about Tiare, how much it had to offer. "There's fresh water, electricity, the airstrip and boat house, a full-time caretaker."

Andy listened, nodding lazily. Mallory saw him paying more attention to her than to West. She frowned at Andy to discourage him from thinking she was just one more party girl. He just winked at her and continued his visual tour of her white Bermuda shorts and sleeveless T-shirt.

West caught the wink, but thought twice about giving the offender a black eye for it. Pitcairn was a client and also a footloose playboy to whom a reflexive wink meant little or nothing at all.

West had to admit he was reluctant to lose face with his old sailing pal. They had played around half the world together on the yacht; they had let the good times roll. And how they had rolled!

How could he explain his feelings about Mallory to Andy? Hell, he could hardly explain them to himself. It was scary to be in love. Andy would laugh him off the yacht.

West went on touting Tiare's virtues, avoiding Mallory's eyes. He hadn't expected to be caught in a face-off between the freewheeling life he knew so well and his unprecedented feelings for Mallory Danner.

"West," Mallory said suddenly, "I'm getting seasick. Would you motor me back to dry land?"

"I will," Andy said, shooting out of his chair.

"Relax," West said to Andy as mildly as he could. "My pilot. My responsibility."

"Don't forget to come back, West," Eden purred as he helped Mallory into the outboard.

Minutes later, on the beach, Mallory faced West. "As you might have guessed, I'm not seasick."

"I guessed, Angel."

"You didn't tell Andy about me over the radio did you?"

"Look, I didn't think it was that important."

"Not important that we're in love with each other? Don't deny it, West. I know how you feel, even though you haven't said so. You haven't had the courage to admit it, even to yourself."

"I've realized it," he retorted. "But I didn't need to put it out on the shortwave."

"If you go back to your old ways, West, I'll never forgive you."

"Angel, I've got to go back to the yacht. Andy's my client. He's going to drop five million for Tiare."

Mallory tossed her chin. "You don't need the commission. You have the millions you inherited."

"Inherited is the key word," he said firmly. "I've learned to like spending my *own* money—money I've earned. Aunt had a lot to do with turning me around about work two years ago. I started selling islands and paying my own way in the world. She was right that I'd been pretty rich and worthless before that."

"Why do you insist on being a playboy, West?"

"I'm just trying to earn an honest income, which requires having a few drinks with my client right now."

"When are you going to tell Andy about us?"

"He doesn't need to know, Angel. I can finesse this whole situation if you'll just stay off my back about 'us.' Now, if you don't mind, there's a party I've got to attend."

Mallory bristled at him. "You're not going to say a word to them? You're not going to tell them that we're more than casual acquaintances?"

"I'm not comfortable about blurting it out like that," he growled. "Not publicly, at least."

"Not comfortable with the serious responsibility that love and commitment require, you mean. Well, I'm not comfortable without it." She turned on her heel.

"Where are you going?"

"Back to the house! Where are *you* going?"

"Back to the party!" He waded to the outboard, leaving his troubles behind him.

AN HOUR LATER, West heard the startling sound of a plane taking off from the airstrip. Standing speechless with surprise on the deck of the yacht, he watched his own twin-engine airplane fly over the yacht and zoom away in the direction of Honolulu.

His plane. His pilot. *Damn it!*

West resolved right then to have all the fun he would have had before meeting Mallory Danner. He raised his *mai tai* in a toast to the captain and crew of *The Party Animal*. "Let the good times roll."

ON THE 747 from Honolulu to San Francisco, Mallory had plenty of time to reflect on what she had done.

Deserting West on Tiare island was the most impulsive, unrestrained, irresponsible action she had ever committed in her life. She didn't feel a bit of regret, either, or have any second thoughts about it.

It served him right!

WEST HAD NEVER HAD a rotten time at a party until the crew on the yacht started living it up and coming on strong. Before Mallory, he would have had a fine time. Now he had the almost uncontrollable urge to cover his eyes as Sable and Crystal tossed their bikini tops overboard and entreated him to get out of his chair and hula with them.

"Not now. I'm sort of seasick," he told them, using Mallory's convenient excuse. Trying to look queasy and green, he stood up and weaved his way to the outboard.

"We'll go with you," said Sable. "We'll take care of you and make you feel better."

West motioned them away. "Stay and keep Andy happy. I'll float back when I feel better."

He sped to the house, almost wishing he'd never met the beautiful butler who had turned his life-style upside down. If he'd never met her or made love to her, he could be doubling his pleasure right now. He wouldn't be a wet blanket.

What was he going to do when the captain and crew decided to bring the party into the house? And how was he going to sail back to Honolulu with them without joining in on the fun?

He'd either have to fake being seasick, or he'd have to party, party, party back to port.

Damn Mallory for putting him in a compromising position!

FIVE DAYS AFTER Mallory returned from San Francisco, she caught the maids in a linen closet, giggling over a tabloid newspaper. The cover photo showed West coming off *The Party Animal* with Andy and the crew in a Honolulu marina. HOT DATE HOTTER THAN EVER! the headline exclaimed.

Ellinor happened by just then and spotted the paper. She snatched up the news and said, "Come with me, Danner. Let's dispose of this trash properly."

Mallory followed Elli to her suite and sat down with her. Elli scowled at the photo and repeated the headline out loud with disgust.

"In spite of this," she said, "I don't give up hope for Third."

"He's hopeless, Mrs. C. He hasn't turned over a new leaf at all. I realize that taking the London job would be the best thing I could do."

"I can't agree," Elli said. "Somehow I feel that Third is ripe to be tamed—by you. How can that happen if you leave him untamed, and how happy will you be without the fun he'll always add to your life? Once he commits, he'll be faithful. Fidelity and fun *can* co-exist."

Mallory shook her head. "Not within West."

"Danner, I'm convinced that the woman who wins him will never regret it. But he must be challenged to commit. Before you run away to London, think of what life without Third will be like for you."

"Mrs. C., I know it won't be a picnic. It'll be . . ." She paused to consider. "It'll be what it was before—efficient, dutiful, responsible, dignified and . . ."

"Confining?" Elli suggested.

Mallory's shoulders slumped. "I'm afraid so. Especially now that West has helped me lighten my serious nature. In fact, without knowing it, he helped lift a burden of guilt from me."

"I don't understand."

"My mother's death," Mallory explained haltingly. "I was playing some silly game with the neighbor kids when she died at home."

"I'm sorry you lost her," Elli said sympathetically. "What made you feel guilty about it, dear?"

"Well, I was supposed to be at home instead of out playing. I sneaked away that day while Dad was reading to Mom and my baby sisters were down for a nap. I'll never forget the look of loss on my father's face when I got home. I should have been there when she died."

"Third told me it was cancer."

Mallory nodded. "Terminal, but Dad kept it to himself. He knew when he brought her home from the hospital that she only had a few weeks left. I didn't know she was on the brink that day. Dad told me not to leave the house, but he didn't say why. I sneaked out and played . . . and never saw her alive again."

Ellinor reached out and squeezed Mallory's hand. "You were just a child."

"I've known that rationally," Mallory confided, "but I've had my problems coming to emotional terms with it. Playing and goofing off made me feel guilty after that."

"You associated it with your mother's death," Elli inferred. "You also had to take on adult responsibilities at a young age, and learned to suppress a part of yourself as you grew up."

"Exactly," Mallory said. "And then I met West. He brought out that part of me, little by little. On Tiare, with him, I learned to stop suppressing it. I even began to think of being his full-time pilot, instead of being a butler. Flying suits me better."

"Give him another chance," Elli urged. "Oh, I know he's reverted this past week, but he has so much potential. Everyone—even West—deserves a second chance."

"I'll think about it, Mrs. C."

WEST FLEW HOME from Honolulu that afternoon. He came in through the back door, unannounced, and found Mallory ready to walk out through the same door.

"Oh," she said, "hello. I was just leaving for a doctor's appointment."

"We need to talk, Angel."

"About the tabloid photo?"

He grimaced. "You saw it."

"I don't want to be late for my appointment, West."

"It wasn't the way it looked, Angel. I didn't really *do* anything, except close the Tiare deal. I made some mistakes on Tiare, sure, but you made some, too. Flying off in my plane without me, for one."

"You're right, West. The plane isn't my property—it's yours. I'm sorry I took it before asking."

"I'll forgive you if you'll forgive me," he bargained, eager to have her in his arms and take up where things left off on Tiare.

She was holding back from an embrace, though. Holding out on him as if she expected more.

"Angel," he said coaxingly, "let's go upstairs and really forgive each other."

"And after we do, then what?"

He spread his hands. "What do you mean 'then what'? We'll keep on having a good time. What else?"

"West, I need more than sex and fun with you. You need more, too, but you won't let yourself see it."

"Look, Angel. You know what I am. You've always known what I—"

"No, *you* look. You taught me to have fun I can never have again without heartbreaking memories of you. You made me love you. But all you can be is a hot date." Walking out the door, she bitterly quoted the tabloid, "'Hotter than ever!'"

West followed her to her car. "Give me a break."

She shook her head. "Give me more than sex and fun."

"Not a word in that sleaze sheet was true," he protested.

"You're making me late for my doctor's appointment," she said, getting into her car.

He grabbed the door handle. "Wait a minute. You're not ill, are you?"

"Yes. Lovesick and heartsick!"

Frowning, West watched her drive away. He turned and saw Elli approaching with Valentine in her arms.

"Welcome back from *The Party Animal,* Third."

"Don't you start in on me, too, Aunt," he said, giving her a kiss. "I've already been chewed out once."

"Dah-dee," babbled Val.

West took the baby in his arms and she immediately started sucking on his shirt button. Emotion flooded him as he looked down into her face. Not long ago, this sweet child had brought Mallory and him so closely together. He couldn't forget playing house with them. He'd loved every minute of it.

"The Party Animal," Elli scolded.

"I did nothing you wouldn't approve of," West protested. "I swear it on Val's innocent heart."

"Even so, Danner will be happier in London, where she can forget you exist. Lord Eaton's butler has resigned and she has been offered the position."

West almost dropped Val. "Angel's leaving?"

"Yes, unless the man she loves stops her with more than sex and fun—if I eavesdropped correctly."

"She refused to believe anything I said, Aunt."

"You wouldn't say what she needs to hear," Elli declared. "Why not?"

West threw up his hands. "I said enough! What more does she need to hear?"

Elli's gaze clouded, became troubled. "Danner hasn't been in tip-top health since the island . . . nausea every morning . . . dizzy spells . . ."

West stared at her, looked down at the love child in his arms, his thoughts whirling.

Elli raised her eyebrows questioningly. "Her symptoms lead me to wonder if you were entirely careful on the island, you scamp. Were you?"

"No," he blurted. "I mean—just once we didn't—I mean—" He was thinking, *That time on the surfboard!*

"Dah-dee," Val babbled.

"My God!" West exclaimed. "Now Angel is preg—and I'm the fath—"

Elli said, "I had dizziness and nausea during my own short pregnancy."

Feeling dizzy himself, West went inside with Val and his aunt to Elli's suite. Suddenly Michelle appeared, pale and upset, interrupting his reverie.

"Alex just called," she murmured in a frightened voice. "Somehow he got the phone number. He said he'd beat me up and take Valentine."

"The hired hands won't let him get close enough," West assured her. "And I'm here now. I can take care of him if he slips through the net."

"He sounded meaner than ever. Vicious."

"Don't let him worry you," Elli said. "We're all here and Danner will be back soon, armed with her gun."

Reassured, Michelle returned to the sewing room with Val, and Rosa and Edith arrived to make Elli's bed and scrub the bath. In the meantime, Elli briefed West on what had happened while he'd been gone.

"The detectives' morning report is that Alex is back in town. Danner began packing a pistol again, just in case." She settled back in her chair. "Now, convince me that that awful tabloid is full of hot air."

"Aunt, you know it is. Not one word was—"

Elli's phone rang, and West answered. It was Odd-job.

"Run to sewing room! Now!" he exclaimed.

"Why?"

"Alex break in—beat Michelle—take baby!"

"Coming," West said tersely. "Stay put."

He cursed and banged down the phone with so much force that Edith and Rosa came running out of the bedroom.

"Alex got in and took Val," he said. "Michelle's hurt."

They all rushed to the sewing room and found Michelle almost unconscious from a blow to the head. Oddjob was kneeling on the floor, holding her.

"I come to visit. I find this," Oddjob explained, cradling Michelle against his chest. His voice cracked. "All beat up. Bastard Alex!"

Michelle whimpered, "He took Valentine."

"When?" West asked.

She blinked her eyes woozily. "Just before Oddjob came in."

Elli picked up the sewing-room phone. "I'll call the police and an ambulance."

Oddjob said to West, "I don't see him come—or go. I just see Michelle. Knocked out."

"He had to get through a lot of the house to get out," West reasoned. "He could still be inside."

Oddjob nodded. "Hiding. Big house."

"He had to park somewhere," West said, "like he did last time." West went to the sewing-room window, where he could view the alley. The blue Mustang he remembered was parked there. He saw Alex running across the back terrace with Val clutched in his arms.

West threw the window open. "Stop!" Alex kept running. West whipped around. "Oddjob, come with me."

Elli and the maids took Oddjob's place with Michelle.

"The police and medics are on their way," Elli called.

West sped down the rear stairway with Oddjob behind him. "Where's Q?"

"Fish market," Oddjob replied.

Bursting through the back door, West saw Alex reach the back gate and shouted, "Alex!"

He could see Alex fumble the crying baby, stumble through the gate then drop her in the middle of the alley. She waved her arms and screamed.

West dashed through the gate and scooped Val up from the ground. The Mustang started up and took off, speeding down the long alley. Something at the end of the alley caught West's eye. He got a shock.

Another car—Mallory's—was stopped across the exit, blocking Alex's way. West saw Mallory get out of the far side of the car and aim her gun over it at the Mustang.

West was stunned. *Where did she come from?*

Mallory could see West in the middle of the alley. The Mustang sped up and she yelled at him, "Get out of range."

He stepped back behind the gate, shielding Val.

Alex was coming straight at her, faster and faster. *He'd be smarter to back up*, she thought, because the other end of the alley was wide open. But blind fury seemed to be driving him forward. He had already proved more than once that violence toward women was his style.

Mallory took careful aim and shot out his front tires. The car slammed to a stop. Alex scrambled out and ran back the other way. She chased after him, then saw West ambush him from the gateway and wrestle him to the ground.

As Mallory came up to them with her gun pointed at Alex, West was hauling Alex to his feet. He held him in a wrenching armlock.

"That's my pregnant wife you almost ran down, you bastard," West growled at Alex. "My pregnant wife!"

Oddjob came through the gate, holding Val. Elli followed behind him.

"Oddjob, Michelle is asking for you," Elli said to him. "Take Valentine and tell her everything is under control."

He shook a fist at Alex, then stepped back through the gate with the baby.

All the while, Mallory was trying to comprehend what West had growled to Alex. *Pregnant wife?*

He was repeating himself as he cranked Alex's arm tighter. "My pregnant wife! I should strangle you on the spot for it."

"West," Mallory said. "I'm not pregnant."

"You aren't?" West glanced at Elli. "But Aunt said you've been dizzy. Upset stomach."

Mallory nodded. "A *tourista* bug I picked up on the island, I suspect. My cycle is fine."

"Oh," both West and Elli responded, looking disappointed.

"I'm also not your wife, West," Mallory added meaningfully.

He started to say something but at that moment, the private eyes he had hired came speeding into the open end of the alley. They jumped out of their car.

Alex sneered, "Late for a date, dudes?"

"Not for your court date," one of them shot back. He looked at West. "I'm sorry we lost him."

West shrugged, quoting Val's bib, "Spit happens."

Alex snickered coldly. "I'll show Michelle not to cross me up. Don't think I won't."

"You need help, Alex," Mallory said. "I had a feeling you were up to no good when I saw you heading this way in your car."

Alex glared at her. "Oh, yeah? Where were *you*?"

"Driving out of the Broadway tunnel," she replied. "You were heading into it, with your radio turned up so loud I couldn't help but notice."

"Too bad you didn't run into a traffic jam, babe."

"I made a U-turn," Mallory continued explaining, wanting to rub it in. "Traffic in the tunnel slowed me down for a few minutes, but not long enough for you to get away." She looked at West. "What happened before I got here?"

"He beat Michelle and almost kidnapped Val," West told her.

"They're mine," Alex boasted. "They'll learn."

Mallory narrowed her eyes at Alex. "You won't be around to teach them anything."

West was looking puzzled. "Your gun, Angel. You took it to a doctor's appointment?"

She nodded. "Not on purpose. I got used to wearing it and forgot it was there."

The police arrived just then and took Alex into custody for assault. They left to interview the private eyes at headquarters. The ambulance medics examined Michelle and determined that she wouldn't need a hospital stay or skull X-rays.

When the hubbub finally died down, Elli called West, Mallory and the entire staff together in the drawing room. After commending them all for their security efforts on Michelle's behalf, she singled out Mallory.

"You were wonderful, amazing. What will we do without you if you go?"

"Without her?" Berthe queried.

Mallory explained about the London job offer. "I'm thinking of accepting it, for personal reasons. And Lady Eaton is—"

"Wait a minute," West interrupted her. "You can't."

"Why not?" Elli inquired.

West frowned. "Well, because I have something to say first. Not in front of everybody, though."

Elli herded the staff out and left West and Mallory alone.

Mallory rose from her chair and faced West. "I don't really want to go, but our situation being what it is, I'm leaning toward taking the job."

"I don't want you to go, either," West said, coming to his feet. "Why don't you lean toward staying, instead?"

"Stay and be another one of your party girls?" She shook her head. "No, West. I wouldn't be happy that way. Maybe that's enough for some women, but not for me. I'd only be happy if . . ."

"If I asked you to marry me?" West said slowly. "Would you, Angel?"

"Don't tease me, West. This afternoon you said, 'I am what I am.' A playboy forever, in other words."

"I was jet-lagged, Angel. And too blind to see I'd outgrown my old ways. Seeing Alex try to kill you— and my future with you—opened my eyes all at once."

"It did?"

"You bet it did. I'm not teasing. I saw you as my wife, pregnant with our child. I saw what I'd lose if I lost you. That did it for once and for all."

"Did what?"

"Made me sure of how much I love you, how much I want to marry you."

Mallory felt breathless. "Are you really sure, West?"

"Without a doubt," he confirmed, taking her in his arms. "I'm ready to be the world's hottest husband— and father, if we decide to have a family."

Mallory sighed. "Well then, I'm ready to be the world's hottest wife, mother—and playmate."

"Will you marry me, Angel?"

"Yes." Mallory replied, and lifted her lips to his.

EAVESDROPPING on the other side of the door, Ellinor smiled to herself. Just as she had expected, everyone would live happily ever after. And soon she'd be a great aunt!

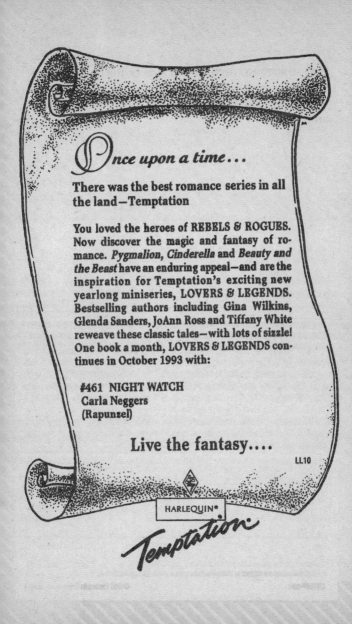

Once upon a time...

There was the best romance series in all the land—Temptation

You loved the heroes of REBELS & ROGUES. Now discover the magic and fantasy of romance. *Pygmalion*, *Cinderella* and *Beauty and the Beast* have an enduring appeal—and are the inspiration for Temptation's exciting new yearlong miniseries, LOVERS & LEGENDS. Bestselling authors including Gina Wilkins, Glenda Sanders, JoAnn Ross and Tiffany White reweave these classic tales—with lots of sizzle! One book a month, LOVERS & LEGENDS continues in October 1993 with:

#461 NIGHT WATCH
Carla Neggers
(Rapunzel)

Live the fantasy....

LL10

HARLEQUIN®

Temptation

Take 4 bestselling love stories FREE

Plus get a FREE surprise gift!

Special Limited-time Offer

Mail to Harlequin Reader Service®

3010 Walden Avenue
P.O. Box 1867
Buffalo, N.Y. 14269-1867

YES! Please send me 4 free Harlequin Temptation® novels and my free surprise gift. Then send me 4 brand-new novels every month, which I will receive before they appear in bookstores. Bill me at the low price of $2.44 each plus 25¢ delivery and applicable sales tax, if any.* That's the complete price and—compared to the cover prices of $2.99 each—quite a bargain! I understand that accepting the books and gift places me under no obligation ever to buy any books. I can always return a shipment and cancel at any time. Even if I never buy another book from Harlequin, the 4 free books and the surprise gift are mine to keep forever.

142 BPA AJHR

Name	(PLEASE PRINT)	
Address	Apt. No.	
City	State	Zip

This offer is limited to one order per household and not valid to present Harlequin Temptation® subscribers. *Terms and prices are subject to change without notice. Sales tax applicable in N.Y.

UTEMP-93R   ©1990 Harlequin Enterprises Limited

FIRST-PERSON PERSONAL

Nothing is more intimate than first-person personal narration....

Two emotionally intense, intimate romances told in first person, in the tradition of Daphne du Maurier's *Rebecca* from bestselling author Janice Kaiser.

Recently widowed Allison Stephens travels to her husband's home to discover the truth about his death and finds herself caught up in a web of family secrets and betrayals. Even more dangerous is the passion ignited in her by the man her husband hated most—Dirk Granville.
BETRAYAL, Temptation #462, October 1993

P.I. Darcy Hunter is drawn into the life of Kyle Weston, the man who had been engaged to her deceased sister. Seeing him again sparks long-buried feelings of love and guilt. Working closely together on a case, their attraction escalates. But Darcy fears it is memories of her sister that Kyle is falling in love with.
DECEPTIONS, Temptation #466, November 1993

Each book tells you the heroine's compelling story in her own personal voice. Wherever Harlequin books are sold.

LIGHTS, CAMERA, ACTION!

Hollywood Dynasty

HARLEQUIN®
Temptation

The Kingstons are Hollywood—two generations of box-office legends in front of and behind the cameras. In this fast-paced world egos compete for the spotlight and intimate secrets make tabloid headlines. Gage—the cinematographer, Pierce—the actor and Claire—the producer struggle for success in an unpredictable business where a single film can make or break you.

By the time the credits roll, will they discover that the ultimate challenge is far more personal? Share the behind-the-scenes dreams and dramas in this blockbuster miniseries by Candace Schuler!

THE OTHER WOMAN, #451 (July 1993)
JUST ANOTHER PRETTY FACE, #459 (September 1993)
THE RIGHT DIRECTION, #467 (November 1993)

Coming soon to your favorite retail outlet.
